MW01034017

Tormenta Isla

By

Lynda L. Lock

Tormenta Isla

your friend
Sparky

and Max

Tormenta Isla

The legal stuff

Most of the characters and events in this book are fictional except the following: Rosa Sirena's Restaurant & Palapa Bar, owners Debbie and Willy Chacon; Villa la Bella B&B, owners Curtis and Ashley Blogin; Apache (Isauro Martinez Junior) and Doctor Delfino Guevera.

Captain Tony Garcia and his fabulous photos of island life are also real.

Any other resemblance to persons, whether living or dead is strictly coincidental.

Tormenta Isla
Published by Lynda L. Lock
Copyright 2018
All rights reserved.
Electronic Book: ISBN 978-0-9936203-6-2
Print Copy: ISBN 978-0-9936203-7-9

Dedication - the things we do for love

To Lawrie Lock, my partner in all things: marriage, life, adventures, and writing.

You are my rock, my inspiration, my sounding board. We've traveled the world together getting into mischief, sticky situations and occasionally heated arguments that typically revolved around a finicky, British car doing something weird. Like the Aston Martin DBS V8 that would just die, without warning, as we happened to be speeding along an eight-lane superhighway in some European country.

Happily our wacky adventures have always ended with giggles and a good story to tell.

So, here's to another thirty-eight years of love and laughter.

Love you to the end of time.

Chapter 1

August 15th

A battered, grey pickup truck trundled toward the southern end of the rarely used airport runway. The paint was patchy, sun-faded and interspersed with areas of rust. Rough usage by the owner had deeply dented the roof of the cab. This was his work vehicle and he frequently carted heavy tree trunks destined to be the main supports of palapas, the large grass-roofed structures commonly used as shelters for restaurants, bars, and swimming pools. Both brake lights on the truck had stopped functioning years ago, but no one cared, not the owner, not his passenger, and certainly not the local police. The headlights worked, intermittently, but on this night, they were purposely switched off.

The main road that circumnavigated the low, narrow island ran on either side of the airfield. Even on a moonless night, the radiance from nearby street lamps allowed the driver to see his way without using the vehicle's headlights. He kept to the edge of the pavement, hoping the overgrown jungle on either side of the landing strip would hide his pickup from curious eyes.

Sunrise was still two hours away, but the island was seldom ever entirely static. There were always either locals returning to their homes after a late night-out, or fitness fanatics hitting the pavement for a run around the island in the cooler pre-dawn temperatures.

To the right of the runway, illuminated by the bright lights of the parking lot, the car ferries waited impassively for the workday to begin. The employees usually started to arrive by four-thirty in the morning. He glanced at the two older Maritima boats. They looked weather-beaten and shabby. Three new yellow and blue Ultracarga ships sat waiting for government permits to commence operation in competition with the existing company.

The driver stopped the vehicle at the far southern end of the pavement, put it in first gear, and switched off the ignition. The wild vegetation pushed ever northward in an effort to reclaim this piece of land belonging to the Municipality of Isla Mujeres. The airport had been operated and maintained for many years by the Quinta Regional Marinas, the 5th Navy detachment, until the agreement was cancelled and the responsibility for the property was returned to the city. Rumours abounded about the future of the land; a housing development planned by a now-disgraced former state governor, condos, even a larger aerodrome to service international jets in conjunction with a cruise ship terminal. Small town gossips created rumours as quickly as two rabbits could produce more bunnies.

He turned to his passenger, "This should work."

"You sure about this?" the other man asked.

"Sure, the Navy guys used to keep this area cleared out, but no one comes here now." The driver pointed at the thick tangle of trees and bushes facing them. "Good thing you wore boots," he said, with a light chuckle. "There could be snakes in there."

"Snakes? Hell, I'm not going in there."

"They are probably not poisonous." He had to take the chance to get rid of his cargo. The vile smell was rapidly becoming noticeable.

The passenger shuddered, and then looked into the bed of the truck. "Alright, let's get this over with."

"Wait," the driver reached up and switched off the interior dome light. "Okay, let's go."

The two men quietly opened the doors and pushed them closed but not completely latched. Noises carried across the open expanse of the airport. A soft click and the driver unlatched the tailgate, and then boosted himself into the bed of the truck. He tugged on a large bundle wrapped in plastic sheeting and wound around with several strips of thick grey tape. He dragged it closer to the other man. "Grab the end," he whispered.

Grunting with the weight, the two men crab-walked to the edge of the jungle.

"Stop." The driver set his end of the roll on the ground. He reached into a pocket and pulled out a finger-sized flashlight, putting his hand over the lens to shield the light but still give him enough to see where he was going. His heavy lion-headed signet ring glinted briefly in the light. "There," he said, pointing a finger at a faint pathway, "it leads to the salina, about ten more feet."

"What's a salina?" the other guy whispered.

"Salt-water pond," the driver grunted a response. They half-carried, half-dragged the heavy load past rusting metal drums containing who-knew-what and a collection of small derelict boats. Fast-growing, thick-stemmed vines with white bell-shaped flowers, a brawny version of the gentler Morning Glory, were beginning to camouflage the mess.

"Any crocs?"

"Don't think so," the driver said, amused at his helper's nervousness. The man was from the City of Puebla and obviously not comfortable around wild creatures. He had no problem dealing with dodgy humans but seemed afraid of all critters.

"There damn well better not be," the passenger whispered nervously as they started again. "There sure as hell better not be any crocs."

"Let's go." Keeping the small flashlight trapped between his palm and the rolled plastic, the driver smiled to himself. There could be a croc living here but probably not. Not much food available for a big reptile except a stray cat or dog, or maybe a wading bird or two. Although, one of those nasty critters would be a big help with disposing of their parcel. They could have taken the package to the lake at the Hacienda Mundaca where there sure as hell were crocodiles, a whole family of them. But that area was too visible and it would have been too hard to manhandle a heavy weight from the road, across the park and into the water. This location would have to do.

Fighting their way along the narrow pathway, the men pushed deeper into the thick undergrowth, until the helper stepped backwards and his boot sunk up to his ankle. "Christ. That stinks," he bitched.

"Okay, set it down," the older man said. He then cautiously swept the nearby shoreline with the beam from the flashlight. "Roll it until the water covers the plastic."

Tormenta Isla

Both men were calf deep in the odoriferous ooze before they were satisfied with the placement of their parcel. "That's not going anywhere," the driver said. "Okay. Let's get out of here just in case there are crocs," he added with a smirk.

Chapter 2

August 16th

Food! It seemed like her life revolved around food. What to eat? Where to eat? When to eat?

Pulling open the refrigerator door, Jessica Sanderson confirmed her suspicions. It harboured only an iffy container of coconut-flavoured yoghurt and a dish of blueberries that resembled raisins, not berries. The litre of skim milk for her morning coffee was reasonably fresh. She had purchased it two days ago, stopping at a neighbourhood tienda after she finished her shift at the Loco Lobo Restaurant & Bar.

The cool air from the open refrigerator felt good. She lifted the blonde plait that hung down the middle of her back. Her thick mane of hair was hot and heavy but she just couldn't bring herself to cut it shorter. It was as much a part of her as her bright blue eyes, her slim physique, and the full-sleeve tattoo on her left arm depicting turtles, flowers, whale sharks, and dolphins.

She huffed out a sigh, banged the door shut, then crossed her arms and leaned against the kitchen counter. Staring at an empty refrigerator wasn't going to fill her stomach. She pulled out a chair and slumped at her kitchen table. Being single sucked.

Single, but not alone, she mused as she reached down to pat her dog, Sparky. When people asked what type of dog he was she usually responded wryly with, "He's a pure-bred island-low-rider."

The responses usually ranged from an incredulous, "Oh, I haven't heard of that breed," to a perplexed, "a what?"

"A mutt," she would clarify with a chuckle, "He's a mix of every dog that has ever lived on this island."

Sparky's curly fur was a mix of black, brown, grey and white. He had a compact body, short legs, a pink-spotted tummy, floppy Spaniel ears, and humanlike brown eyes. His front feet were larger than his back feet, and he loved to dig. His nose was legendary, having uncovered a stash of pirate treasure at the Hacienda Mundaca almost a year ago; a stash of gold, silver and jewels that she and her best friend Yasmin Medina had searched for and found, only to have it claimed by the Mexican government.

"For the people of Mexico," the authorities had said. At least she and Yassy hadn't been thrown in jail for treasure hunting without a permit; a permit which was impossible to obtain but still required by law.

Her stomach rumbled, reminding her of a more pressing problem; no food in the house and she was hungry. What she really wanted to do was to stop by Villa la Bella B&B to indulge in one of their famous Piña Coladas or Cadillac Margaritas. She could sit at the swing-bar, listen to Jimmy Buffet songs, and have a little visit with Curtis and Ashley before going to work. But they didn't serve food and she was famished.

If there was another person consistently in her life she might be tempted to buy groceries and actually cook a meal or two. She and her current love interest, Luis Aguilar, dated occasionally. He was one of the island's notarios, a career in Mexico that had a higher status in the hierarchy of lawmakers than a lawyer. They enjoyed a romantic, but uncommitted relationship that had started a few months ago as a joke over an iguana.

The iguana had somehow found its way into a sewer drainage vault near the Loco Lobo on Hidalgo Avenue. The fat reptile had blocked the flow of liquids, causing a smelly flood at street level. When the Aguakan employees freed the creature, Jessica had offered to relocate it somewhere safer.

Luis had been standing nearby and joked about iguanas tasting like chicken when they were barbequed. She was quite certain her sexy smile had convinced him to help her carry the container holding the stinky and unhappy reptile four blocks to the empty lots near the Poc Na Hostel. Fastidiously clean, Luis had hesitated only briefly before cheerfully agreeing to help. In exchange for his assistance, she agreed to have a drink with him on her next day off.

Jessica sighed and picked up her cell phone to call, yet again, one of her favourite neighbourhood eateries that offered a delivery service.

"Bueno. Kash Keken Chuc," a feminine voice said in a breezy island-style greeting.

"Buenos Días," she replied.

"Is that you Jessica?" the voice asked.

"Si, Amelia, it's me," she replied with a laugh in her voice. "I need food."

"A quarter chicken with all the fixings?" Amelia asked, referring to their popular meal of charcoal-grilled chicken that came with beans, rice, coleslaw, tortillas and hot sauce, all delivered for just under five dollars.

"Yes, the same order as Friday please."

"Gracias, Jessica," Amelia said, "talk to you in a few days, chica."

"Gracias a ti, Amelia." She disconnected. Putting her phone on the kitchen counter, she said to Sparky, "I have to get a life. The staff at all of my favourite take-out places know what I am going to order." He didn't answer; he only offered tail-wagging agreement.

Currently her culinary efforts extended to preparing special meals for her pooch to accommodate his dietary requirements. He was born with a genetic glitch, an enlarged heart, and he had recently developed a problem with elevated enzymes in his liver. The local veterinarian had suggested she cook Sparky's food for him and not feed him anything pre-packaged. However, boiling up a pot of chicken, sweet potatoes, peas and carrots for her pooch didn't do anything to sharpen her cooking skills for herself.

She also supplied chopped fruits and vegetables to the lounge of lizards in the garden. She'd read that amusing expression on YucatanLiving.com. A group of lizards was called a lounge. So, she supposed, a group of lizards hanging around could be thought of as a lounge of lizards lounging in a lizard lounge.

Oh-kay then, she really was spending way too much time by herself.

While waiting for the delivery of her order, Jessica scanned through the on-line local news stories. They were all in Spanish and frequently she only got the gist of the article, but it was slowly improving her comprehension of the language.

Tormenta Isla

Today's headline was something about a missing taxi driver, Ricardo Villarreal Garcia. His empty vehicle had been discovered parked by the cemetery near the Guadalupana colonia, the newer and larger graveyard on the Caribbean side of the island. The tiny original cemetery in Centro, crammed between new hotels, condominium developments, and homes, was over-loaded with departed souls. The new one was at least a dozen years old but rapidly filling with large tombs for the islanders who had recently died.

Jessica didn't recognize the name of the missing man, thankfully not one of her friends. The island had so little crime, other than the frequent theft of small electronics and cash; it wasn't likely that anything bad had happened to him. Perhaps he was ill and had gone into the bushes to be sick, or empty his bowels. Presumably, someone had searched the area in case he had fainted or had a heart attack. With any luck, he had already been located and the news reporters hadn't updated the situation.

Nothing else on-line caught her attention, so she clicked on the television for background noise and flipped to the weather channel. It was a continuation of the usual late summer weather, hot, sunny and humid with late-afternoon rain showers. Off the coast of Africa, a yellow X on the weather map indicated that a disturbance was forming in the Atlantic Ocean near Cape Verde. It could mean heavy rains and high winds in about ten days to two weeks, or it might just disappear altogether.

She hoped the disturbance would dissipate and not interfere with the upcoming national fiesta. September 16th was Independence Day in Mexico, equal in importance to July 1st in Canada and July 4th in the United States. The celebration would start with the politicians re-enacting the 'Cry of Delores' at midnight, followed by fireworks, ringing of the bells and the crowd shouting: Viva! Viva Mexico! Just thinking about the energy from the crowd caused goose bumps to lift up the fine blonde hairs on her forearms. She was Canadian through and through, but she had backpacked across more than thirty countries since she graduated from high school nine years ago, and the pride and enthusiasm the Mexican people displayed on their national holidays was always a thrill. It never got old.

But the real reason she wanted the weather to stay calm, September 16th was also her twenty-seventh birthday and she planned to celebrate with the usual crowd of close friends, Yasmin, Carlos, Pedro, Diego, and his wife Cristina. And Luis, yes definitely Luis.

Chapter 3

August 17th

Yasmin Medina's sparkly sandals clicked on the stamped concrete floor. Her long, lean legs carried her inside the cool interior of the Loco Lobo where she was the assistant manager and head bartender. She felt good. She was twenty-nine, in love, happy, and healthy. Life was perfect.

Her mass of dark curly hair bobbed in sync with her strides, the light bouncing off the natural blonde highlights that ran through her tresses. Yasmin strongly resembled a famous island woman born in the 1860s. Martiniana Gomez Pantoja, nick-named La Trigueña or the brunette, also had sea-green eyes and dark blonde-streaked hair. Martiniana was the Mayan teenager that the Spanish sea-captain-turned-pirate Fermin Antonio Mundaca de Marecheaga lusted after. The one-sided love affair never flourished. The younger woman spurned the attentions of Mundaca, who was thirty-seven years older, and instead married her childhood sweetheart.

Yasmin's short pleated skirt swung in rhythm with her walk. She loved how the bright orange and pink patterned skirt, paired with her pale orange top, making her feel so fresh and tropical. She waved hello at the other employees before heading straight to Carlos Mendoza's office at the back of the building.

"Hola mi amor," she said, wrapping her arms around him as he sat at his desk. He slowly stood up, keeping her close to his chest, and kissed her deeply.

"Nice!" He said, before loosening his intense embrace just a little.

"Um hmm, very nice. What are you up to?" her arms looped around his neck, she peered around his shoulder to see what he was working on.

Keeping one arm wrapped around her slim form, he flipped his free hand in the direction of the stack of papers. "Verifying invoices and paying them if they are correct. Same old boring stuff."

"The exciting life of a respectable businessman." She said referring to the recent incident where Kirk Patterson, an escaped killer who was wanted for several murders in Florida, had kidnapped Carlos. Patterson was seeking revenge against Carlos for turning him over to the American authorities after Kirk had threatened to kill Yasmin. The situation had been triggered when Yasmin, Jessica, and her dog Sparky had discovered the cache of pirate treasure the previous November. Patterson wanted it. Carlos and his buddies prevented him from getting it. Carlos was held captive for four days while Patterson attempted to grab Yasmin. Fortunately, their friends Diego, Pedro, Antonio, and Sparky, engineered his rescue and their lives returned to normal.

The kidnapping had happened just as she and Carlos had decided to take the first tentative steps along the road to romance. They didn't need that kind of excitement in their lives. Now eight months along in their relationship they were happily in love, although still keeping separate residences. They enjoyed their frequent sleepovers, as Jessica jokingly referred to her nights spent with Carlos.

She leaned back and let her eyes roam over him. At thirty-nine years old he was middle-aged handsome, muscular and lean with deep brown eyes, black hair, and café au lait skin. A faint scar ran from his left eyebrow to the corner of his mouth, a souvenir from his wilder younger years. His smile swept across his face and crinkled his eyes, turning her insides to sizzling mush. He was hot! Oh, mama, scorching hot.

Carlos motioned to the other chair in his office, "Stay and chat with me for a minute."

"I can't," she pulled a sad face, "I have a very demanding boss. He insists we start work exactly on time."

"Don't worry. I'll have a talk with that cranky bastard. Sit, please."

Yasmin lowered herself to the chair and crossed her legs, showing off her toned thigh. "What would you like to chat about?"

"Nothing really, just wondering if your mom and dad are coming back to the island for the Independence Day festivities?" he asked.

"I don't know," her eyebrows pinched together. Her parents had moved a few years ago to the City of Mérida to be nearer their older daughter Adriana and their only grandchildren, six-year-old Eduard and eight-year-old Enrique. Yasmin and her forceful mother Maria Victoria Guzman de Medina had a loving relationship, at a distance. Victoria wanted more grandchildren and she couldn't understand why Yasmin was not married. When her mom started one of her you-are-almost-thirty crusades, her sweet papi just smiled and gave his younger daughter a loving hug.

"Why do you want to know?" Yasmin asked, puzzling over his question. She crossed one arm across her middle and propped her chin on her closed fist.

"I thought maybe we could celebrate together. You and I have been spending so much time together I would like to meet your parents, your sister and her family."

Tormenta Isla

"Mi amor, I've been working here for almost four years," she said, sweeping her arm to indicate the restaurant outside his office. "They know who you are."

"I know, but I would like to get to know your family better."

She studied his face. *What brought this on?* "Okay," she shrugged, "I usually call Mom every other day, so I'll ask her tomorrow if they are coming to Isla for September 15th and 16th."

"Bueno!"

~

"You did what with him?" the thick-set man snarled.

"Dumped him in the salina," answered the taller man. He was bone-thin with ropy muscles created by the heavy physical work. His pants hung on his lanky frame, bunched at the waist by a worn leather belt. A gold ring glinted on his right hand. It was a prize taken several years ago in Guadalajara from the hand of another dead man, a souvenir of his first kill.

"*Madre de Dios!*" the other man swore. "The salina is a favourite place for dog walkers and joggers. The dogs will smell him."

Tormenta Isla

"No, no. Not the Salina Grande," the thinner man responded. He shifted his weight, his work boots scuffing the ground. "The one at the end of the airport runway, behind the gas station." Dark eyes devoid of any expression stared back at him. He wanted to glance down to break eye contact, but that would indicate fear. It was best to meet the glare of a dangerous predator square on.

"When I told you to deal with the problem, I meant deal with it, not re-locate it."

"Don Rafael," he said, respectfully using a Spanish honorific title of 'Don' instead of just calling the man by his first name, "no one will find him. The airport is nearly abandoned, only used rarely when the Navy helicopter or the state governor is visiting the island." He could feel the prickle of sweat on his back and smell the stink in his armpits. He stilled his body, concentrating on not panicking. The man sitting across from him had personally killed dozens of competitors and ordered the disappearance of dozens more.

"For your sake, I hope you are right, Edgar," Rafael Fernandez said, staring flat-eyed at his subordinate. "I truly hope you are right."

Chapter 4

August 18th

Stripped down to shorts and deck shoes, Pedro Velázquez and his brother-in-law Diego Avalos were catching up on small maintenance jobs on their jointly-owned charter boat. The fifty-eight foot Viking, *La Bruja del Mar*, the Sea Witch, was berthed behind the Bally Hoo Restaurante, at the wharf known as the Isla Mujeres Yacht Club, or the Lima docks. Her well-maintained twin twelve-hundred horse MAN diesels, made by Maschinenfrabik-Augsburg AG in Austria, always ran sweet and steady, but they had been putting off the gritty little jobs. They had a few days of downtime, with no new photography or fishing charters on the books for three weeks, so it was a perfect time to scrub the decks, polish the metal, and change the oil and the filters on the engines.

Thirty-seven year-old Pedro strongly resembled his Mayan ancestors, with his short stocky build, wide-shoulders, long torso and thick powerful thighs. His face, with its blade-like nose, hooded deep-set eyes, and sculpted lips could have been the model for the ancient statues at the Mayan temple of Chichen Itza.

Tormenta Isla

His brother-in-law Diego was one year older and taller, with longer legs and finer features that hinted at a touch of Spanish blood in his veins. His often-broken nose marred his otherwise handsome face, giving it a slightly menacing look until he smiled. Then his infectious grin and easy laugh made everyone want to be his best friend.

Pedro's shaved head glistened with sweat in the morning heat. Mid-August, the middle of hurricane season, was always hot and humid with little or no wind. "Did you look at the NOAA site today?" he asked, referring to the American operated National Oceanic and Atmospheric Administration that tracked developing weather systems.

"Si, two disturbances out there now. What was a yellow X has been upgraded to Tropical Storm status. That one's been named Pablo." Tropical storms and hurricanes were given human monikers to make it easier for the world at large to track on news channels and internet sites. Until 1979 all named storms were given feminine tags, until pressure from activist groups convinced NOAA to alternate between male and female names.

"I noticed that," Pedro said, "plus the one following is now a red X." This meant the second weather system had been tagged by NOAA as having a higher probability of developing into a cyclone, normally called a hurricane. "I have already confirmed our normal emergency berth at the Makax Marina."

"Good. If things deteriorate in the next few days we can move the boat." Diego held up his hands to show Pedro that they were filthy from working on the engines. "Can you toss me that rag?" he said, indicating one of his old ripped t-shirts that had been turned into a wiping cloth.

"Catch," Pedro said as he tossed the shirt towards Diego. It was an inexpensive give-away handed out like penny-candy to the crowds during the recent campaign for Presidente de Isla Mujeres, or as their English-speaking friends would say, the Mayor.

Diego said, "This storm, Pablo, is tracking straight across towards the Leeward Islands, then it is supposed to turn north." He scrubbed the t-shirt over his hands, removing most of the grease and oil.

Pedro countered with, "It isn't that strong. Maybe it will die out once it hits land." Pedro resumed his task of buffing the railings.

"Claro," agreed Diego. "It's odd how the tormentas that cause so much damage along the eastern coast of Central and North America are formed off the coast of West Africa."

"If I remember correctly, it's something to do with the winds of the Sahara blowing in wave-like motions over the desert then slamming into the moist air near the Cape

Verde islands." Pedro was rubbing at a stubborn bit of corrosion on the railing and stopped talking for a moment before continuing his explanation, "it takes the right combination of heat, moisture, and updraft to create a thunderstorm." He stood back to scrutinize his work, then resumed polishing. "When the thunderstorms form clusters we get the potential for a hurricane."

"Well aren't you the science whiz-kid," teased Diego.

"Si, I loved the subject in school."

"Okay smart guy. What's the old Carib name for the God of Evil?"

"Hurican."

"Correct answer. Here's your prize," he said, tossing the filthy rag at Pedro, who snatched the cloth out of the air and stuffed it into a metal pail.

Diego picked up their maintenance 'to do list' and crossed off the tasks that they had completed. "Only four more things on this list, then we're done."

"I just hope all this cleaning and scrubbing we're doing isn't wasted." Pedro was silent for a minute or two thinking about something else that had been niggling at the back of his brain. "Did you see that bit on TV Isla Mujeres about that missing man? Ricardo Villarreal Garcia?"

"The one whose empty car was found near the new cemetery?" Diego said.

"Yes."

Diego shrugged his shoulders, "I don't know him. Do you?"

"No," Pedro said, "but I might have seen something going on between him and two other guys."

"Really? What did you see?"

"I'm not sure if it is the same guy because I didn't look at the number on his cab," Pedro said.

"What happened?"

"A couple of days ago I saw two Mexicanos, driving a beater of a truck, swing in front of a taxi and slam on the brakes. It happened so suddenly the taxi driver almost rear-ended the other vehicle. The two men got out and accosted the driver, one on either side of his car. They were shouting, pounding on his windows and trying to wrench open his doors," Pedro said.

"His doors were locked?" Diego asked. "That's unusual."

"Yeah, now that I think about it strangely enough they were. I've never known a taxista to lock the doors, especially in broad daylight. He must have been anticipating trouble when he saw them."

"Do you remember anything about the guys?"

Pedro offered a wry grin, "Sure. Dark hair. Dark eyes. Dark skin," he said referring to the gibe that from a distance all Mexicans looked alike, "and tall like you."

"Not me. I'm innocent," laughing, Diego held up his hands. "Maybe you should report the incident to the cops," he added.

Pedro quirked his eyebrows up, giving Diego a skeptical look.

"Filipe Ramirez is a decent guy. Tell him."

Chapter 5

August 19th

A dark blue police cruiser pulled to the curb in front of a one-story unfinished concrete block casa. Two men stepped out, shutting the doors but leaving the car running and the air conditioning on for the two constables sitting in the back. The senior man was trained as a firearm specialist and had a pistol secured to his utility belt. The majority of the municipal law enforcement officers did not carry guns, although a few were taught to use Tasers.

He lightly tapped his knuckles on the unpainted wooden door, causing it to rattle against its loose frame. "Señora Villarreal?" he called out.

"Who is it?" asked a tremulous feminine voice.

"Policiá. Sergeant Ramirez. Open up please." The door opened a crack exposing a dark, gloomy interior. The officer could only see one brown eye and a slice of her cheek through the meager opening. "Buenos Días, Señora Villarreal. May we come in?" he asked, his hand resting lightly on his gun.

"Why?"

"We have a few questions about your husband's disappearance. It would be better to chat in private."

"I'm not feeling well," the woman complained.

"I understand, Señora, but you want us to find your husband, don't you?"

"Si," she grudgingly agreed as she moved away from the door.

The senior man stood on the threshold while warily pushing the door wide open. "It's dark inside, Señora. Please turn on a few lights." He held his left hand out, indicating to his younger partner to stay outside until he knew what they were walking into.

"The light gives me a headache."

As his eyes adjusted to the gloomy interior, Ramirez could see that the woman had been beaten. She had a black eye, a cut on her nose, and several dark bruises on her arms and face. "Yes, I see. Just turn on one light please," he said firmly.

She reached out and clicked a wall switch, weakly illuminating the space with one bare fluorescent bulb hanging from the ceiling. She instinctively turned her damaged face away from the light.

"Thank you." Turning towards his younger partner he quietly said, "Tell Alexis to join me," referring to the policewoman who was sitting in the back of the cruiser. "You can wait in the car."

A few minutes later a woman asked, "You wanted me Sergeant?"

He nodded, then said to the other woman, "Señora Villarreal, this is Constable Gomez. May we come in?"

The woman sighed resignedly, "Alright, come inside. Sit down please." she said, pointing at a couch.

Ramirez entered first, his hand reflexively skimming the butt of his gun. The stench of cat urine made his eyes water.

He caught the look of distaste as Alexis surveyed the filthy interior, her eyes coming to rest on the piece of furniture the woman wanted them to sit on. It was thickly covered in pet hairs, particles of food, and a sticky residue that might be a spilled soft drink. The mulish look on her face said she wanted to remain standing.

"Thank you," Ramirez said, lowering himself then eyeing his subordinate until she begrudgingly complied.

He tilted his chin towards the older woman, indicating to Alexis that she should ask the questions; woman to woman might get honest answers.

~

Alexis warily perched on the edge of the sofa with her small notebook and pen balanced on her knees. She began quizzing the woman, "Señora Villarreal have you heard from your husband?"

"No," the woman snapped, wincing as she exhaled. "I would have told the police if I had."

"How did you get so badly injured?" Alexis asked, softening her voice. She could see the woman was supporting the right side of her torso. She had her left hand tightly pressed against her ribs and her right elbow clamped securely over her hand. It was a sure sign that she had at least one or more cracked ribs.

"I fell."

"When?"

"Yesterday."

"Have you been to a doctor?"

"No, I'm fine."

"You might have broken a rib or even two. You should go to the hospital for x-rays."

The woman defiantly glared at Alexis with her one good eye, "I said, I'm fine."

Tormenta Isla

Alexis scanned the cramped accommodations, noting a partially used bottle of blue nail polish, a discarded pair of Spiderman shorts, and a pink t-shirt too small for the woman sitting in front of her. "Do you have children, Señora?" she asked.

A light sheen of sweat covered the woman's face as she gingerly licked her swollen lips. "Si," she whispered, "a son and a daughter."

"Where are they now?"

"Visiting my mother, "the woman replied, her eyes aimed at the filthy floor.

"Do they know you are injured?"

"Leave my children out of this!"

Alexis flicked a glance at Ramirez, silently asking if she should press the issue. He lightly shook his head.

She changed her line of questioning, "Señora, do you know of anyone who recently threatened your husband, or had a grudge against him?"

"No, my Ricardo is a decent, god-fearing man."

Oh yeah, salt of the earth I'm sure, Alexis thought to herself as her eyes skimmed around the hovel-like interior of the house. "We've had a report that your husband was seen in an altercation a few days ago in Centro. Do you know anything about that?"

The woman's face froze, the blood draining away from her face turning her skin a pale latte colour. "No," she stammered, her eyes sliding to the side. "I don't know anything about that."

"Two men driving an old grey pickup truck were seen pounding on the roof and pulling on the doors of his taxi, trying to open them."

Refusing to meet the younger woman's probing gaze, she reflexively shook her head, wincing at the pain. "I don't know anything about that," she repeated weakly.

After restating their questions in a variety of ways and not getting any useful information, Ramirez and Alexis thanked the woman for her time and exited the house.

"Well, that was a wasted effort," Alexis said, pulling at her shirt. After twenty minutes of sitting in the cramped, foul-smelling shack, her uniform was plastered to her back with sweat.

"Not entirely," Ramirez said, "we now know she is terrified of someone or something."

"True, but what or who is she afraid of?"

"That's what we need to find out. In the meantime let's get someone from the DIF to do a check on her and her kids," Ramirez said, referring to the National System for Integral Family Development, the Mexican institution tasked with providing social assistance for families. "I want to know those kids really are with their grandmother, and that they are okay."

"Give me a couple of minutes and I'll make the call," Alexis said, twisting to see the seat of her pants she batted at her uniform, dusting the crud from her butt. She caught the sergeant grinning at her. "What?"

"Can I help you with that?" Ramirez asked.

"*Pendejo*!" She retorted, discreetly displaying her middle finger.

He chuckled showing brilliant white teeth. "Constable Gomez, you need to learn to respect your senior officer."

"And you Sergeant Ramirez need to understand who is really the Jefa," she said, using the feminine form of boss, then winked at him. "By the way, it's your turn to cook tonight."

Chapter 6

August 20th

"Well shit," Diego said.

"Diego, the children." Cristina pointed at their four young children sitting at the breakfast table. She wagged a forefinger at him, reminding him not to swear within hearing range of their young ears.

His two middle youngsters, Pedro Junior and Luisa, chanted in unison, "Papi swore. Bad Daddy." Ana, their youngest, giggled loudly behind her hands. She was too young to know why it was funny, but her older siblings were laughing so she imitated them.

"I'm sorry. Please excuse me for swearing," he said, smiling at his wife and the kids. "It's a very bad habit."

His oldest son José, who was turning eleven in October, replied, "It's okay Papi. It was a very bad mistake but we forgive you."

Diego smiled at José. He had become so serious, so grownup after his Tio Carlos had been kidnapped. Carlos was not genetically José's uncle, but in Mexico close friends were considered to be part of the family. Diego still worried that his son might be suppressing his anxiety but he seemed fine, and the child psychologist agreed that he was coping well.

"Thank you, José. I appreciate your forgiveness."

"You are very welcome, Papi."

"What upset you, mi amor?" Cristina quietly asked. She took a damp cloth and wiped Ana's sticky fingers and face, then lifted the toddler out of her high chair and set her on her lap. She peeked inside the baby's diaper, and then smooched Ana several times. "Yum, yum. You taste so good I could eat you up!" she said, causing the tot to giggle and squirm.

Diego held up his smartphone and silently showed her the screen, pointing at the NOAA graphics. He studied her face, still so beautiful after all these years of being married to him and bearing their four incredible children. His love for her deepened with every passing day. Her smile could still squeeze his heart with love.

Cristina's eyes opened wide in surprise as she looked at the screen, then a frown crinkled her brow. "Really? Three?"

"Si, Pablo, Rebekah, y Sebastien."

"Mama, who are those people?" José asked, his head cocked to one side as he studied his mother's face. "Do we know them?"

"No, mi amor. They are just visitors who hopefully will either change their travel plans or won't stay long," Cristina answered. Diego could see she was forcing a smile, attempting to reassure their always inquisitive son, José.

~

"Is today your day off?" Luis Aguilar asked as he rolled over in bed to face Jessica, one hand lightly tracing the curve of her cheek.

"Yes, it is," she said. "Do you want to do something together?" She gazed into his gorgeous dark-brown eyes. A person could get lost in those pools of melted chocolate.

"Sure," he said, pulling her closer. He kissed her forehead, then her nose, then her lips, and was headed further south when she put a hand between his searching lips and her hot skin.

"I meant something other than spending the day in bed," she said, lightly slapping his gorgeous bare butt.

"It is a healthy activity. Sex is a great cardio exercise."

"Yes it is," Jessica swung her feet out of the bed, and stood up, "but you have a business to run, Señor Aguilar." She said pointing at him and then at her bathroom. "Shower. Now."

"It's Sunday. I don't work on the weekends." He propped himself up on one elbow, letting his eyes roam over her naked form. "Come back to bed. I need more exercise."

"Go," she pointed again, pretending to be serious. If he didn't get into the shower soon she was going to hop back into bed and screw his brains out.

"Spoil-sport." He pulled back the covers. "It seems a shame to let this go to waste," he said, looking down at his erection.

"It's not like those are rationed," Jessica retorted with a grin.

"Sure they are. It doesn't happen every time."

Jessica's eyebrows quirked up, "Really? Well every time we are together it does, more than once."

"Then let's try for a new record."

Two hours later Jessica slipped out of bed a second time. Yes, they had set a new record, and now she really needed to pee, plus she was starving hungry and thirsty. Luis appeared to be asleep but she locked the bathroom door as a precaution. He loved to sneak in while she was showering to help soap her sensitive bits, and that invariably led to more sex in the cramped enclosure. She thought she had a vigorous libido, but the guy was insatiable. She needed to revitalize herself with food and a couple of glasses of cold water.

Plus Sparky was undoubtedly doing the pee-pee dance by now.

"Hey, you locked the door," he said, rattling the door knob. "I have to take a leak."

"Tie a knot in it. I'll be out in fifteen minutes," she replied, as she stepped under the cascade of warm water, "or open the back door for Sparky. He'll show you a good spot to use," she shouted over the sound of running water.

Having successfully showered without any assistance from Luis, Jessica relinquished the bathroom to him. "Your turn," she said, dancing past his hands as they reached to loosen the towel tied around her slim frame.

Stepping into the small space and turning on the shower, Luis tossed an invitation over his shoulder, "why don't you join me?"

"Nope, I'm hungry," she retorted, "for food."

Munching, Jessica looked up from her late breakfast, or was it an early lunch of toast slathered with creamy-style peanut butter. She watched Luis strut naked from the bathroom into her bedroom. He smiled crookedly at her as he pulled on his clothes.

"What do you want to do for dinner tonight?" he asked.

"Order in I guess?" she said. Breaking off a small piece of toast, she held it out to Sparky. He sniffed and turned his head away. "Divo!" she said, laughing at his fussy eating habits. "I know, I know. It's not filet mignon."

"Are you kidding me?" Luis said, as he watched the dog refuse the treat Jessica was offering him. "Any other dog would have wolfed that down in three seconds flat."

"I know. I know. He's finicky."

"Finicky! More like spoiled rotten," Luis said with a laugh.

"My house, my rules," Jessica said, putting the chunk of toast back on her plate and wiping her fingers on a paper napkin. Behind her back, Luis rolled his eyes. He was certain he saw Sparky smirk at him, giving Luis the doggy equivalent of a one finger salute.

"Alright then," Luis said catching her not-so-subtle hint to butt out, to mind his own business. "Why don't we try that new place, Rosa Sirena's?"

"The Pink Mermaid? Where is it?"

"Near Mango Café and Caribbean Brisas but on a side road. They also have a bar on the top floor," Luis said. He zippered his pants and buttoned his formerly neatly-pressed linen shirt. "We could go for drinks first, then have dinner and come back here for dessert," he suggestively waggled his eyebrows up and down.

"Luis Aguilar, you are a hopeless sex maniac," she said, laughing at his comical expression.

Chapter 7

August 21st

Jessica waved at Yasmin as she entered the Loco Lobo. A few months ago they would have arrived at work together, but since Yassy and Carlos were an item, things had changed. The couple were so engrossed in each other that Jessica and Yasmin usually only had a chance to chat on the phone, or at work, and only when the restaurant wasn't crazy busy. She was very happy for both of them, but she missed their girlie evenings spent with a bottle of wine and a pizza, watching a chick flick or two.

"How have you been?" Jessica asked, giving Yasmin a light hug and a buss on the cheek.

Yasmin returned the gesture, "todo bien. You?"

"I'm good," she responded with a wry chuckle. "I've been busy entertaining Sparky," she said, then added softly, "and Luis."

"Entertaining Luis?" Yasmin said, her eyes twinkling with laughter. "I can just imagine. That would include a lot of indoor exercise."

"Hey," Jessica retorted good-naturedly, "we went out for dinner last night."

"You didn't order in? Amazing."

"We went to a new place, Rosa Sirena's."

"Carlos mentioned that yesterday. He said his friends Deb and Willy just opened it recently." Yasmin glanced around the quiet restaurant; no customers yet. "How was it?" she asked, turning back to Jessica.

"Fabulous! Good food, romantic setting and the desserts, oh-my-god-to-die for! I had a yummy Crocodile cocktail." Jessica licked her lips, "It's named after that big crocodile, the one you call Alfredo."

Yasmin laughed at the memory of their treasure hunting episode at the Hacienda Mundaca Park the previous November. "Remember the gate attendant, Adela Yam? She would point at Sparky and tell you that the crocodile liked to eat small well-fed dogs."

"Yeah, I remember very clearly her weird sense of humour," Jessica said, with a dry laugh.

Yasmin shook her head, grinning at Jessica's expression.

"I guess I had better earn my money and get busy." Jessica glanced around the restaurant, looking for customers. No one yet! Mid-August to the end of September was traditionally the slowest time of the year for tourism, and she, like many of the islanders, relied on visitors for their income. Tips for wait-staff, bartenders, tour boat operators, and hotel staff were a welcome supplement to the standard wage.

"Have you been watching the NOAA site?" Jessica picked up a damp cloth and started to wipe down table tops.

Yasmin nodded and gave a little shudder, "Yes, it's worrisome. Three tormentas mid-Atlantic and so far they are all tracking straight towards us."

"I chatted with Diego earlier today. He says they will perhaps turn north when they get to the Leeward Islands, but by that time the first storm will be just a couple of days away," Jessica glanced at Yasmin, checking to see if she agreed with Diego's assessment.

Yasmin was nodding, "That's pretty common, although not always the case," she said.

"Which hurricanes were you here for?"

"I was only about a year old when Gilberto arrived so I don't actually remember it, but Dad said it arrived mid-September of 1988. It was a category five and did a terrible amount of damage to the island."

Tormenta Isla

"I've seen old photos with a freighter on the beach near the ruins of a hotel."

"Si, Gilberto destroyed the Perla Hotel, knocked down all the power poles, and cut a deep channel through the main road on the Caribbean side of the island. We didn't have any electricity for weeks. The island was pretty empty. All the visitors left."

"No tourists, and trying to recover from a hurricane. That must have been hard for everyone." Jessica had been shocked when she first started working on Isla, and was told about the ridiculously low daily wage. The Mexican national rate was around five dollars American per day. Per day for heaven's sake! Tips were the only way to make a decent living. No wonder the slowest month for tourism, September, was referred to as *Sept-hambre* by locals. It was the month when they were frequently hungry.

"It was a very difficult time for the islanders."

"When did the other hurricanes happen?"

"Let me think. The next one happened when I was in grade three," Yasmin replied, "so...that would make it 1995. Yes, I remember now, October 1995. It was called Roxanne. It was a lot less destructive than Gilberto."

Jessica said, "I don't remember much about the more recent hurricane, Wilma, other than it was a bad one. I was a self-absorbed teenager living in a small Canadian town and I didn't pay much attention to anything other than what was going on with my friends and family." Jessica smiled at the memory of being fifteen, and in her mind, the centre of the universe.

Yasmin snorted a laugh, "I wasn't much better. I was seventeen at the time, but it was pretty hard to ignore Wilma. She was another monster that slammed into Isla in October 2005."

"I've seen photos on the internet."

"There are some pretty dramatic images," Yasmin agreed. "Normally a hurricane will pass by within four or five hours, but that one stayed for almost three days. It did huge amounts of damage especially in the Cancun hotel zone."

"Broken glass everywhere, I imagine," Jessica said.

"Structural damage too. The winds were unrelenting. Most of the concrete balconies on the oceanfront hotels were ripped off."

"Are you kidding me?" Jessica asked, glancing at Yasmin to see if she was joking.

"No, it's the truth. I remember my dad saying more than a hundred hotels on the Mayan Riviera were unable to re-open. Many had serious structural damage and had to be torn down and rebuilt."

"That must have caused a lot of financial hardship."

"Yes," Yasmin agreed, "but the Mexican government threw everything they could at the problem. Workers. Money. Assistance. The hotel zone was partially re-opened in time for the winter tourist trade. The full recovery took a few years but at least there was some money coming in to rebuild the economy."

Yasmin pointed a finger towards four people who were settling themselves at a table. "Finally, customers."

"Hi guys!" Jessica called in her cheeriest voice, as she picked up four menus and walked towards them.

"Welcome to paradise."

Chapter 8

August 22nd

Cristina Avalos anxiously tapped her freshly-decorated acrylic nails on her kitchen table. The tiny green, white, and red Mexican flags, painted on her fingernails, glimmered in time with her fidgeting. The source of her unrest was the television weatherman dramatically proclaiming the three tormentas were still on track, headed towards the Caribbean Sea. It was irritating how he sounded so ridiculously cheerful, as if he was looking forward to reporting on the destruction of other people's lives.

The internet and television weather reports were mixed as to the eventual destination of the Pablo, Rebekah, and Sebastien. Some said the first storm would turn at the Leeward Islands near Martinique and set the path for the two smaller cyclones, pulling them north along the American coastline.

However, the majority of the stations were forecasting the first tormenta to strike Venezuela then turn into the Caribbean Sea and hit Nicaragua, Belize, and Mexico, again dragging the other two behind. Nothing was ever certain until the storms were closer, much closer. Even then a non-threatening category one cyclone could rapidly build into a roaring monster and then just as suddenly diminish to a tropical storm. Her brother, Pedro, said it all had to do with water temperatures, wind directions, land temperatures, and adjacent high or low pressure systems.

She had lived thirty-five years, her entire life, without evacuating for a hurricane, and there were many factors that she had no control over. She did, however, have some control over the safety of herself, four small children, and one large husband, Diego.

Thankfully they didn't have any pets to worry about. The kids were constantly pestering her for a puppy but she was holding firm, no animals. She had plenty of daily chores without the added stress of keeping track of a young dog. She knew it would rapidly become her responsibility as soon as the children realized that pets continually required food, fresh water, exercise and training. They were too young to stay focused on caring for a pet.

The home that she and Diego owned was compact, and tucked in between the two adjoining houses on Calle Fragata in Colonia Miraflores. The area was marginally higher than the surrounding area and offered some protection from flooding. Rainfall during a tormenta could be a frightening two meters in one day, more than Diego's height.

The small rise in the land allowed the rain to run downhill into the two nearby bodies of water; the Salina Grande on the eastern side of her neighbourhood, and Bahia de Mujeres the bay between Isla and the mainland on the western side. Her friends who lived on the edge of the Salina Grande would likely experience flooding. There was a massive pump designed to lower the water level in the landlocked pond, but, of course, it required electricity to operate and sometimes even the backup generators did not function properly.

Her parents lived in the same neighbourhood and they were typically well prepared for anything. Her brother, Pedro, was currently single and he frequently stayed overnight, enjoying their mom's amazing cooking. Between her parents and her brother she was confident they would be well organized, but just in case she decided to confirm they were prepared.

She called her only sibling. "Hola hermanito," she said using the diminutive of brother.

Pedro's deep voice purred in her ear, "Hola Chiquita. Que pasa?"

"Are mama and papi ready for the hurricane?"

"Si, we have been working on the house today. Everything's done."

"Are they stocked up on bottled water, canned goods, and non-perishable foods?"

"Cristina, this isn't our first time." His rich laugh made her smile. She loved her brother as much as she loved Diego and wished he could find happiness with a partner.

"I know, I know. But I worry about them."

"You have your own family to worry about. Are you ready?"

"Si, we have our supplies and a few treats for the children." Eager to prove to her older brother that she was as competent as he was, she continued reciting her list. "The Jeep and my moto are gassed up, and I took extra cash out of the bank, in small bills." In the past the municipality had deliberately cut off the electricity to prevent fires and electrocution from downed wires. The bank ATM's couldn't operate without power, debit cards and credit cards were similarly useless in stores.

"Me too," Pedro said. "I'm sure your kids are excited to be out of school tomorrow."

"Oh yeah, thrilled, until they discover there is no internet, no television, no electricity, and no water pressure other than the slight dribble from the roof-top storage tank." she said, thinking about the boring and stressful days or weeks ahead. The schools would close soon and stay closed until everyone could return to normal routines. The kids would be over-joyed, especially José who was at best a reluctant student. Food could still be prepared on the stove while the propane lasted, but cold drinks would run out as the refrigerator warmed up. If the storm was severe it could take weeks to restore electricity and begin the process of normalizing their lives.

"Is the house boarded up?"

"Tomorrow. Diego purchased two sheets of plywood yesterday. He has to cut them to size and cover our windows."

"Good. I can help him."

"He plans to nail the back door shut, and once we are inside nail the front door closed as well. I don't trust the hinges and locks to hold against the wind."

"Okay, I guess that's reasonable," Pedro said, sounding as if he thought otherwise.

Ignoring the tone in Pedro's voice she asked, "How about the boat?" She was referring to *La Bruja del Mar*, the big sport-fishing boat that her brother and her husband co-owned. Worth several times more than their house, they couldn't afford to lose it. Even with hurricane coverage the insurance companies were notoriously slow to pay, preferring to deny compensation entirely. Her stomach cramped with acid indigestion. She hated hurricanes. No, not just hated them, she detested them.

"Don't worry. It's all organized. We're going to move it tomorrow or the next day at the latest," he said.

Chapter 9

August 23rd

Feet up on his desk, Carlos leaned back in his swivel chair, checking his ever-growing list of things to do if the hurricanes didn't turn north. Twelve years ago when Wilma battered the island he was a free man, no house, no restaurant, and no fancy 911-Porsche to worry about. He hadn't even been married to his thankfully now, ex-wife Elena. His only concern then had been to protect the family home and his dad's *panga*. The small fishing boat had been the main source of income for the family, and still provided income for his parents.

His siblings, Nicolas, Roberto, and Marianna, now all lived on the mainland in the Valladolid area with their families. They were well away from the ocean and the danger of storm surges that increased the depth and force of the waves. The wind might hit Valladolid, but historically the city had seldom suffered damage from hurricanes. They would look after themselves. If the tormentas turned west, he had the family home, his business, his house, Yasmin's house and Jessica's house to secure. Diego and Pedro would help where they could but they had their own responsibilities to worry about.

Ordering fresh meat and vegetables for the Loco Lobo would get complicated. The trick was to have enough on hand to serve customers, but not get caught with a cooler full of perishables if, or more likely when, the electricity went out. Anything that could float or blow away would have to be secured. The staff could stack all the restaurant furniture against the back wall and tie everything together, and pack as many of the small items as possible inside the walk-in cooler. He scrubbed his hand over his face. How did life get so complicated?

"Hey, Carlos? Are you in?" a familiar voice asked as the owner rapped a knuckle on his office door.

"Hi Luis, come on in," he said as he swung his feet off his desk and onto the floor.

"Que pasa? What's happening?" Luis Aguilar asked, giving Carlos a palm-slap fist-bump greeting.

"Planning for the worst, hoping for the best."

"Si, me too. I have *cortinas* for the two windows and the entrance door at my office, and that just leaves my apartment." He glanced out at the restaurant. "Do you need some help here?"

"Not here, but Jessica or Yasmin could use some help."

"Jessica, of course I'll help her," Luis grinned.

"*Pícaro*. What have you been up to?" Carlos asked, teasing his friend that he was a randy horndog.

"Me?" Luis asked innocently. "Nothing," he answered.

Carlos laughed.

"Okay … changing the subject," Luis said with a chuckle, "I keep seeing items in the local papers about the taxi driver, Ricardo Villarreal. It's been almost a week and he's still missing."

"Do you know him?"

"Only slightly. He and his wife, Rosa, were in a few months ago, asking me to do a small piece of legal work for them," Luis said, with a shrug of his shoulders. "Nothing complicated, they asked about getting their wills prepared."

"Wills?"

"Of course, everyone should have a one. I suggested that they wait until September because then it's half-price for Mexicanos to have their Testamentos drawn up."

Carlos said, "And now he's missing."

"Yes, and if he is dead that will leave his widow in a big mess."

Carlos' eyebrows quirked up, "Why?"

"No Testamento. Legally the Mexican government can sell everything and distribute the money to whichever heirs they decide should benefit."

"But don't spouses automatically inherit?"

"No, not necessarily. If there are surviving children they might get the money, and the spouse could potentially be completely disinherited."

Carlos stared thoughtfully out of his office window into the restaurant. "I don't have any children, so, if I died without a will … who inherits my stuff? My house, my car, and the Loco Lobo?"

Luis shrugged, "perhaps your siblings. Maybe your parents. Or after an expensive legal battle, possibly even Elena."

"Elena!" he sputtered. "We were only married for three years. I divorced that crazy witch a long time ago." In January Elena had come back to the island to visit her mother. Not realizing that Carlos had been kidnapped, she decided to pop over to say hello, her excuse being she hadn't seen him since their divorce. When he didn't answer the door she tried the front door key she had never got around to removing from her key ring. It still worked. It had deeply shocked him when Pedro said she had been inside his house, as if she still owned half. He had immediately arranged for new locks.

"She could put a claim on your estate as being your helpmate to your success and all that."

"I need an appointment with you, pronto!" he hoped like hell that she hadn't been fingering through his personal papers or bank statements. They had settled everything fifty-fifty in the divorce, when he was a much poorer man.

Luis laughed. "Yes, you do," he said, "I'll get my assistant Alicia to email you with a time and date. Got to get back to work, see you later." He waved goodbye.

~

Luis smiled to himself. He still didn't know anything more about what had happened to Ricardo Villarreal, but it had been fun winding up Carlos over Elena. Mentioning an ex-spouse from a particularly rancorous divorce was usually a great way to generate more revenue, especially on the wills and testaments side of his business, although Carlos really did need to get a testamento registered.

Tormenta Isla

He pushed open the door to his notario office on the corner of Juarez Avenue. "Alicia?" he called, when he didn't see her at her desk.

"Si, Señor Aguilar?" she replied, poking her head over the metal railing that separated the narrow stairway from the mezzanine storage area.

"Could you please email Carlos Mendoza with a choice of times and dates for an appointment."

"Claro que si. How much time will you need with him?"

"Only about an hour. We are going to prepare his testamento."

"Bueno."

"And Alicia?" he said, craning his head back to see her face, "we need to get ready for the storm that's coming."

Chapter 10

August 24th

Sparky woofed once to let her know that someone was outside, obviously someone he recognized since his tail was rapidly wagging back and forth.

"Hola? Anyone home?"

"Just a minute. I'm coming," Jessica hollered as she scurried towards the knocking.

"Hi Jess," Luis said, leaning in to give her a kiss while Sparky sniffed his ankles.

Enjoying the amorous smooch, Jessica reluctantly broke it off long enough to pull him into her house and away from curious stares. "Come inside," she said, closing the door, then she pressed her frame against his and re-ignited the passionate lip-lock, her hands freely roaming his trim physique.

"Whew," Luis said, as he pulled away and tugged at the front of his trousers.

"Your *gonchies* a little tight, honey?" she asked using Canadian slang for men's briefs.

"They must have shrunk in the laundry," he replied, yanking at his underwear until he was comfortable. "Not to ruin the moment," Luis said, "but I just chatted with a group of firefighters, the guys who double as the civil defense volunteers. They are inspecting neighbourhoods for potential problems like large loose items. Rodrigo, the fire captain, said Hurricane Pablo is now a category three and it is headed this way."

"Well, that sucks," she said, moving away from the doorway and settling in the kitchen. "How soon before it gets here?"

"Three or four days, maximum."

She tugged on her thick braid, pulling the heavy weight over one shoulder, "What's the wind speed?"

"It's about two hundred kilometers an hour," Luis said, "and that makes it close to one hundred and twenty-five miles per hour, in the American measurement."

"I'm Canadian," she said, reflexively correcting him, "we use metric."

"Oh, right. I forgot."

"Yeah, I know. All pale-skinned foreigners look like Americans." She tweaked a smile at him.

Luis grinned self-consciously, "Well you have to admit there are an awful lot of blonde, blue-eyed American women who vacation on the island." He reached down and ruffled Sparky's long silky ears.

"Yep, Minnesota and Wisconsin, even Texas and California seem to produce mostly blondes," Jessica said. He was right, there were a lot of American females who were fair-haired. "Well, I'd better get organized," she said, pushing herself upright.

"I'll help."

"Thanks babe. First priority, I'll need plywood for my windows. Diego said the lumber depot will cut it to size for me, if they aren't too busy."

"I know the manager, Jorge. He'll make sure it gets done."

"Now where the heck did I put it?" Jessica muttered to herself as she pulled open her kitchen catch-all drawer and pawed through her collection of hand-tools. "Got it," she said, holding up her handyman-sized tape measure. She reached for the notebook and pen that she kept on top of the microwave. The scribbler contained her to-do-list and shopping list for the rare occasions when she actually bought food, most of which was for Sparky.

Measuring the height of the window from inside the frame, she jotted that number down. Then she checked the width and made a note of that figure.

"It will be quicker if I help," Luis said, lifting the tool from her hands. "I'll measure. You write."

Fifteen minutes later Jessica stuffed the bit of paper in her pocket, grabbed her phone and keys, and locked her front door. Luis handed her a helmet and she fastened it on her head. Then she boosted her butt onto the back seat of his moto, letting her hands rest lightly on her thighs. She had never been on a scooter until moving to Isla, and it still seemed odd to her that it was easier for the driver to maneuver if the passenger didn't cling to their body. Even so, it was so very tempting to reach forward and caress between his legs, just to see if he could keep his mind on driving. She giggled at the thought of explaining an accident caused by sexual interference.

"What's so funny?" Luis asked.

"Nuttin' honey. Nothing at all."

He gave her an odd look then gunned his moto and headed towards what was locally known as the lumberyard. It was a compact, garage-sized bodega crammed floor to ceiling with an assortment of wood ranging from furniture-grade tropical Zapote to multi-purpose sheets of utilitarian plywood.

At least a dozen people were already lined up with bits of paper in hand. Jessica waved at several acquaintances, people that she knew slightly from the restaurant or from her neighbourhood.

Tormenta Isla

There was an air of urgency and the stirrings of anxiety in the group. Since moving to Isla Mujeres almost four years ago, she had been struck by the seemingly endless patience of Mexicans. They good-naturedly waited for whatever it was that they needed; filling a gas tank, buying food, waiting for service in a store, taking money out of the bank, or lining up for a taxi. This group was abnormally fidgety. They restlessly bunched near the service counter like cows sensing an imminent thunderstorm and nervously pressing against a fence.

Luis whispered to Jessica, "Give me your note, and wait here."

Her eyebrows twitched together, "Why?" she asked, as she handed him the scribbled list of numbers.

"I'll go chat privately with Jorge." Avoiding eye-contact with the harried counter staff, Luis sidled through an unmarked door.

~

Pedro strode up the dock, through the Bally Hoo Restaurante, and opened the door to his Nissan truck. It was parked behind the PeMex gas station on Rueda Medina Avenue. He had intended to fill his fuel tank, but by the look of things the service pump employees were swamped with customers. He turned the Nissan around in the tight space then pointed it towards the street. A glance over his left shoulder confirmed his first assessment. A long line of vehicles stretched from the station north towards Jax Bar at the corner. Nearly two full city blocks of cars, trucks, and a huddle of motos were slowly jockeying towards the two service pumps. He shrugged and decided to try his luck with the bigger station on Aeropuerto Road. Maybe the lineup wouldn't be as bad there.

It wasn't just vehicle drivers who were looking for fuel, but also the moto drivers. Islanders commonly purchased twenty pesos at a time in fuel, either for their motos or for lighting the charcoal used for cooking meals. It was a nuisance for the gas stations, but an accepted practice. It was a common sight to see drivers balancing a recycled plastic bottle on a knee while driving one-handed, headed home with enough fuel to cook the family meals for a day or two. Money was tight for most families. They subsisted on their Saturday to Saturday weekly payday.

A few minutes later he crested the slight rise near the abandoned airport tower and could see a line of traffic on the straight stretch of road. He eased his foot onto the brake pedal, slowing as he decided whether or not to get in line or leave it until tomorrow. This station obviously had the city contract as the first ten vehicles were garbage trucks, municipal trucks, and police cruisers, including their four big motorcycles. Then came an array of private cars and more motos. He glanced at the gauge on his dashboard. More than half a tank, but the truck was a gas hog and he didn't usually let the needle fall below the halfway mark. He sighed and swung in behind a grey truck.

Pedro studied the pickup. It was the same dented, sun-bleached truck that the two men had jumped out of to harass the taxi driver. He stopped, tapped the gearshift into neutral with his foot firmly on the brake, and reached for a pen in the console. He felt around for a scrap of paper while keeping his eyes on the men inside the vehicle ahead.

Flicking his eyes to the bumper of the truck, he scratched a few notes.

Ford. About a mid-1980s F150. State of Veracruz license plate USB 874 D.

The traffic edged ahead a car-length and stopped. Pedro moved a bit closer, hoping to get a look at their faces, but both men faced forward. They seemed to be studying the police cars ahead. Then the driver pulled his Ford out of the lineup and warily made a U-turn, heading back towards Centro. Interesting. It appeared as if the men were avoiding the police.

Again, Pedro tried to get a better look at the driver but the man had a baseball cap pulled down low on his forehead, and his chin was tucked into his chest as if he was trying to hide his face. The only thing he could see was a scruffy, whiskered chin.

He folded the piece of paper and tucked it into his back pocket. He might pass the information along to Ramirez the next time he saw him. Although, he didn't know for sure that the two men were involved in the disappearance of the taxi driver, and pointing a finger at someone just wasn't his way. In Mexico, when a person was imprisoned on suspicion of committing a crime, it was difficult to regain their freedom. He didn't want to falsely accuse innocent people.

He and Diego had been involved in a few dicey activities over the years, including last November when they gave Kirk Patterson, an American murderer, an unsolicited boat ride back to the Florida Sheriffs' Department. It was kidnapping, but in their minds justifiable kidnapping. They were ridding the island of a nasty guy who had threatened Yasmin, and they were helping the American cops recapture a convicted killer.

He tapped his fingers on the steering wheel, thinking. Should he give the municipal policía a description of the grey truck? The lineup moved. He eased the truck forward, creeping closer to the gas station.

Chapter 11

August 25th

The neatly coiffed weatherman pointed to the radar map of the Caribbean Sea displayed on CNN, "Hurricane Pablo is now an extremely dangerous category five storm, packing winds in excess of one-hundred and eighty-five miles per hour," he said, his eyes glinting with excitement. "It is expected to hit Barbados tomorrow, then continue west towards the islands of Aruba and Curaçao. The coastal cities in Venezuela, Colombia, Trinidad, Tobago, and the Grenadines are all under a hurricane advisory."

Jessica chewed at her thumbnail as she listened to the man drone on about the impending disaster. She spit out a piece of fingernail and muttered, "This is bad, really bad."

Sparky lifted his head, then shifted from laying near her feet to leaning against her legs. His ears were down and his eyes were pinned to her face. The tip of his tail fluttered uncertainly; he looked worried.

"It's okay little man," she said as she reached down to hoist his muscular weight into her lap. "I'll look after you. I promise sweetie."

Her ringtone announced a call from Yasmin. She shifted Sparky's body to free up one hand. "Hi Yassy."

"Hi Jess, did you see the recent weather report?"

"Yes, I'm watching it on CNN now."

"Carlos has hired someone to board up his place and my casa today, then the restaurant tomorrow. They'll do your windows after they do mine."

"No need, thanks. Luis and I boarded up yesterday and brought in my outdoor furniture," she said. "I'm all good."

"Oh okay, that's good. I'm moving over to Carlos' tomorrow and we would like you to join us. He says it is easier to keep one place safe than worry about three houses."

"I've got Sparky to think about, Yassy," she said, ruffling his fur. "He needs access to the garden for pees and poops, for as long as we can manage it."

"Jess, you don't want to be on your own during a hurricane," Yasmin said, with a note of pleading in her voice. "Lock him in your storage area with food and water. He'll be fine."

"No, I am staying here with him," Jess said.

"Jessica," Yasmin snapped, "don't be ridiculous. This is a category five. You have absolutely no idea what that means."

"I am staying with my dog," Jessica said firmly, then disconnected the call.

Her hands were shaking as she laid the phone on the coffee table. "How dare she tell me to leave you behind?" she said, staring into Sparky's deep-brown, and very human-like eyes.

Her phone played the ring tone again, but Jessica sent the call to voice mail. A few minutes later it rang a third, then fourth, and fifth time before falling silent. Still trembling with anger, Jessica looked at her watch. Dammit. She had to be at work in two hours and she really didn't want to argue with Yasmin at the Loco Lobo. Carlos would certainly support Yasmin's demands that she move in with them. She didn't want to get into a fight with her best friend and her boss, especially in a public place.

Trying to distract herself, she flipped through her incoming emails. There was a recent one from her parents. Oh crap! She hadn't thought to contact them and they were likely very worried. She clicked to open the message:

Tormenta Isla

Hi honey. We couldn't get through on your phone. It was busy. We are watching the news about Hurricane Pablo. When will you be leaving the island? Do you need money to rent a car or to pay for hotels? Or we will pay for a flight home for you. Whatever is best for you sweetie. Call us as soon as you can. Love Mom and Dad

Oh hell. She slumped on her sofa, hugging Sparky to her chest. It would be so easy just to run back home to Canada, but from May to October dogs were not allowed on airplanes. The weather was too hot for them to sit in cages on the tarmac while the planes were loading or unloading. Too many dogs had died and the airlines refused to take animals in the summer months. So that option was out. Renting a car and driving further inland? Possible, but to find accommodation that would take a dog for a few days, that might be a problem, but it was worth looking into.

She set Sparky down beside her on the couch, and began to search for affordable car rentals and hotels with rooms available in the inland cities of Valladolid and Mérida. She wouldn't mention she had a dog until later, much later. With any luck they would never know.

~

Carlos watched Yasmin pace back and forth in his kitchen. She was waving her hands in the air and shouting as she vented frustration. Her best friend had refused to listen to her advice and had hung up on her. Jessica wouldn't answer her phone, and instead of being in their own neighbourhood where Yassy could stomp down the street and bang on Jessica's door to have it out, she was stuck at his house a couple of miles away. He could offer to drive her there, but he was hoping that if he left it alone for a while both of them would calm down.

Sure he would prefer it if Jessica stayed with them, but he also understood her not wanting to leave her dog behind. Unfortunately his house didn't have a fenced area for Sparky, and turning a dog out onto the street to have a pee during a hurricane was guaranteed to frighten the animal into running away. Running towards injury or death.

He massaged his forehead, pushing at the headache forming there. He got up and casually sauntered towards the bathroom, quietly locking the door for privacy. He scrolled through his phone for Luis's name and waited as the call rang through.

"Hey Luis, it's Carlos. Maybe you can help me out with a little problem."

Chapter 12

August 26th

The big engines of the fifty-eight foot *La Bruja del Mar*, the Sea Witch, purred through the protected waterway of Laguna Makax. The salt-water lagoon was ringed by small marinas backing onto the busy streets of Rueda Medina and Sac Bajo.

Pedro steered the Sea Witch towards their emergency berth at a marina set deep in the inlet. His brother-in-law, Diego, busied himself with sorting out fenders and lines in preparation for docking. A flotilla of boats scurried to safety behind them, creating choppy wakes that jostled the vessels already secured in their berths. All ocean activities had been suspended by the harbour master until the danger had passed. Even the smaller Navy search and rescue boats were being moved into a sheltered dock.

"Hola Angel," Pedro shouted as he eased alongside a slower catamaran tour boat.

Angel Poot waved a greeting then pointed at Diego who stood on the back deck of the Sea Witch, his feet were comfortably braced and his hands resting on a railing.

Tormenta Isla

"Who's the scruffy deckhand?" Angel shouted across the gap between the two vessels.

Grinning, Diego waved a middle-finger salute to Angel.

Pedro glanced over his shoulder at Diego, "a tramp I picked up on the docks. He needed money for tequila." he shouted across to Angel.

Angel laughed, and waved goodbye as *La Bruja* passed his catamaran.

Within the next twenty-four hours the car ferry and the passenger ferries would stop service to the island until the storm had blown through. Anyone who planned to evacuate had to be off the island by tomorrow afternoon. The passenger ferries were routinely berthed deep inside Laguna Makax alongside the tour boats and small *pangas*. The shallow-draft, unwieldly car ferry and the large Captain Hook make-believe pirate ships would be the last to moor in the lagoon. They were normally secured crossways in the entrance as a breakwater for the smaller vessels. The inlet would be jammed by the time all the boats were stored, with captains avoiding the muddy centre of the bay, preferring to tie up to the trees lining the shores. An anchor dropped in the mud would drag in the expected high-velocity winds, pulling the hapless water craft into danger.

"Pedro," Diego shouted.

Pedro glanced back. Diego was pointing at a derelict hull pushed deep into the mangroves on the bank opposite the Varadero Cuban Restaurante.

"Remember that one?"

Pedro nodded, "Si. It broke free during Wilma and smashed into four other boats before it ended up there." Even though this was the safest location for their cruiser, things could still get ugly. Wilma had been a category five hurricane, and she had remained stationary over the island and Cancun for a record-breaking sixty-two hours. She left the shores littered with sunken wrecks, and more than a few were still visible twelve years later.

Pedro throttled the engines back, reducing his speed as he carefully picked his way through the busy waterway. Maneuvering their big boat was a little dicey with the sheer number of vessels moving into the lagoon. He knew the men, and Sarah, the only female captain, were experienced operators who were desperate to save their boats. Their vessels were the main source of income for themselves and their families.

"Listo? Ready?" Pedro shouted.

"Si." Diego waited while Pedro powered *La Bruja* backwards into the slip, then he stepped off onto the wharf, wrapping the stern line around a cleat. Pedro reversed one engine, pulling the big vessel parallel with the docks, and Diego secured the bowline.

"Bueno." he said, giving his partner the thumbs up. Pedro shut down the engines.

Pedro and Diego worked in a habitual and familiar sequence, attaching additional lines to the bow, stern, and sides, and to the cruiser beside them. They stowed anything that could become an airborne missile and secured hatches. Fenders were placed between the hull and the dock, but if the wind was fierce, they wouldn't prevent the dock from scraping against the exterior. Specially fitted canvas covers were pulled over the windows.

Walking the length of *La Bruja del Mar*, both men re-checked their work, tugging on the ropes and tweaking the positions of the fenders. "I guess that's it then," Pedro said, reluctant to actually leave the boat to fend for herself.

Diego nodded, "We've done all we can, she'll survive or she won't," he said stoically. "I've got Cristina and the kids to worry about."

"Si, I know." Pedro patted the shiny hull, "Stay safe carina," he murmured affectionately, then followed Diego. "I'm going to be with my parents. I want to be on hand in case any problems arise at their house."

"Good idea. By the way did you ever contact Ramirez about the guys you saw hassling that taxi driver?" Diego asked, his deck shoes thudding on the concrete wharf.

"Yes, I did, about a week ago. I guess I forgot to tell you."

"Did he find out anything?"

"Sort of," Pedro said, rocking his hand from side to side in the gesture for *más ó menos*, more or less, "he said he visited Villarreal's wife and discovered she had been worked over by someone."

"Worked over? As in beaten?"

"Yes, black eye, big nasty bruises and possibly a couple of cracked ribs."

"She tell him who did it?"

"No, she said she fell." Pedro made air quotes, as in no one believed the woman's excuse.

"A lot of weird things are happening lately," Diego said, digging in his pocket for the keys to his Jeep. He and Pedro had driven there earlier in the day in both of their vehicles. He'd left his at the marina, and got a ride in Pedro's truck to the docks behind the Bally Hoo Restaurante, where their boat was normally berthed.

"Unfortunately, Isla isn't the sleepy little fishing village of our childhood anymore. We have a lot of new-comers, and we're close to Cancun and all of its big-city problems.

Tormenta Isla

"I've been hearing rumblings that two drug cartels are in a territory fight over Isla," Diego said as he put his right hand on the steering wheel and used it to lever himself into the Jeep.

Pedro shrugged a wide muscular shoulder, "No idea. It could be true. Drugs are available anywhere in the world, and plenty of travellers like to use them."

"Sadly, that's true." agreed," agreed Diego.

Pedro pulled open the passenger door and hoisted his muscular physique inside the Jeep. "The weird thing is I saw that same pickup two days ago at the PeMex on Aeropuerto. They were in line for fuel, then changed their minds and left," he said, then remembered he hadn't done anything with the vehicle description that he had scribbled on the back of a Chedraui receipt.

Diego popped one shoulder in a half-shrug, "maybe they didn't want to wait that long."

"Or, they noticed the cop cars ahead in the lineup." Pedro stuck his hand into his back pocket, and pulled out the mashed piece of paper.

"Cars? More than one?"

"The entire fleet, including the motorcycle cops," Pedro said, "I asked the pump attendant about it. He said only one person has the authority to sign for all of the municipal vehicles, so everyone arrives at the same time every day." He unfolded the receipt and turned it over. The description was still readable.

Diego flashed a wide, toothy smile, "Good to know, if we ever need to do something a little bit naughty." He started the Jeep then pointed his chin at the scrap of paper in Pedro's hands, "What's that? A grocery list?"

"No. The make, model and license plate number of the truck."

"Are you going to pass it along to Ramirez?"

"Si," he said hesitantly, still not completely convinced he was doing the right thing.

Chapter 13

August 27th – late afternoon

Jessica strode into the Loco Lobo and coolly waved at Yasmin. Yesterday had been a day of forced smiles and overly-polite conversation between them. Everyone's nerves were already frayed from worry about the imminent storm, and the tiff between the two women had only added to the stress.

By mid-evening of the previous day the two women had patched up their quarrel. Although neither one had changed her mind, they had agreed to respect the other's viewpoint. In Yasmin's family a pet didn't have the same value as a human. In Jessica's world she and Sparky were equals. It was a social distinction that couldn't easily be resolved, so the women agreed to just accept the difference in opinions and move on.

In the meantime there was still a lot of storm preparation to be finished at the Loco Lobo, in between serving the occasional customer. A half-dozen or so acquaintances popped in at various intervals to speculate about the wind speed and Pablo's predicted path. There was still a faint hope that all three hurricanes would turn north in the centre of the Caribbean, bypassing the island. Flooding caused by excessive rain and towering waves would be damaging enough without the high velocity wind.

Carlos had placed a small television in one corner of the granite countertop, to keep everyone advised of the situation. The current reports showed that the two smaller storms, Rebekah a category three, and Sebastien a category two, were beginning to veer to the north as they approached Martinique.

Relieved at the news, Jessica whispered a thank-you to a host of deities from several cultures, including Mayan, Hawaiian, and Hindu, hoping someone was listening. She even tacked on her invented childhood favourite, the Great Goddess of Kitty Cats who was in charge of all animals. Two storms down, and one to go, but the nasty one, Pablo, was still on course to ram the island.

The few remaining tourists who hadn't evacuated wandered around in a daze, finally realizing they were now stuck on an island that was little more than an inhabited sandbar, with a major hurricane headed their way. Notices, in both English and Spanish, had been posted in the last three days recommending immediate evacuation. Municipal employees and civil protection volunteers had visited all of the hotels and advised tourists to leave. Most did. A few didn't.

Tormenta Isla

Jessica had decided against leaving. It was just too darn complicated with Sparky. Many of her island friends had never evacuated for anything including Wilma in 2005, so she was staying. She would be a true islander. Her parents had been less than thrilled at her decision to remain, but in the end what could they do? They lived five thousand miles away and she was a very independent person. She was few days short of turning twenty-seven and had been living on her own since she had graduated from high school.

Tucked into the side of her bra, her cell phone vibrated. She pulled it out and checked the display. Luis. She wouldn't normally chat while working, but there weren't any customers at the moment.

"Hola, sweet cheeks," she said, cocking a hip against the table where she had been removing condiments and menus, in preparation for stacking furniture at the back of the restaurant.

"Hola Jess."

"What's up?"

"I was wondering if I could stay with you," Luis said, "my tiny apartment feels claustrophobic. The windows are covered with plywood. No light, no fresh air."

She had snorted at his disclaimer, "Carlos put you up to this, didn't he?"

"No, no. I just thought it would be more fun if we shared the experience," he said, with an extra emphasis on the word fun. "We can ride out the storm together," he added.

"Ride out the storm together," she repeated, laughing at his sexual innuendo. In the end she had agreed. Luis was level-headed but also funny and light-hearted. He made her laugh and it would be good to have company.

"Okay, stop by the restaurant and I'll give you my spare key."

"I'll be there in a few minutes. I'm locking up my office as we speak," he said, as the screech of a storm shutter being pulled closed echoed in Jessica's ear.

And right on time he sauntered into the Loco Lobo. "Hey beautiful," he said, leaning in to give her a quick smooch.

Holding her closed fist against her chest she tightly clutched the key. "This isn't permanent. This is only until the storm blows through," she said.

"Si, si. I understand. I have my own apartment," he agreed. "Should I stop at the grocery store and get supplies?"

Her eyes fastened on his devastatingly gorgeous smile. She decided that a couple of nights stuck inside her house with him wasn't going to be too much of a hardship. "No, I'm pretty sure I have enough of everything we need, unless you have a favourite beverage or snack you want."

"I'll take my stuff over to your place, check on the pooch, and then pop to the store if I think of anything we might need."

"Could you please let Sparky into the backyard for a pee-break, refill his water dish and give him a scoop of his special food?"

"Sure, no problem," he said agreeably. "Where do you keep it?"

"In the fridge, in a plastic container with his name written on it. The scoop should be sitting right beside it," she said. "Oh, and don't forget to microwave his meal for fifteen seconds so that it smells more appetizing to him."

"Heat your dog's dinner?" his eyebrows popped up in surprize. "Really?"

"Yes, really."

"Okay," he said, a grin tweaking his lips. "Do I pass the test? May I have the key, please?" he held out his hand, palm up.

She smiled, "Alright, alright. I guess you are trust-worthy enough to look after my dog."

"Thank you," he said, folding his hand around the key, "I'll come back at closing time and pick you up on my moto."

~

Tormenta Isla

"Spooky," Jessica said, a few minutes after midnight as she was locking the security grill at the Loco Lobo. The streets were dark. The stores were closed. Most of the late-night bars had already shut down. Windows and doors were covered with whatever was available in an attempt to prevent the glass from exploding inward with the force of the wind. She and Luis waited a few seconds for their eyes to adjust to the blackness, then using her cell phone as a flashlight, cautiously walked towards his motorbike.

Sliding onto the back seat of the moto, Jessica glanced skyward at a break in the clouds. "Look at the stars, Luis!" she exclaimed. "They're breathtaking."

He paused and tilted his head back, "Just like when I was a little kid, before Cancun got so big and polluted the nighttime sky with light."

"When I was little and lived in a small rural town, the stars were bright there too. I miss that," she said wistfully.

"Me too," Luis said, "ready to go?"

"Yup, all set."

The island seemed to be hunkered down, holding its breath and waiting for the arrival of Pablo. A tense energy filled the dark and empty streets. Houses, stores, and restaurants were boarded up, or the accordion-style hurricane shutters, *cortinas*, were pulled tightly across openings. In the absence of those higher-priced safeguards, windows were criss-crossed with packing tape to reduce injuries caused by shattering glass.

Luis' moto sped past a police truck with just two constables inside the cab, not the usual contingent of three in the front and another three or four perched on metal benches in the bed of the truck. Jessica wondered if the others were on the mainland looking after their own families.

Many of the police personnel lived on the continental part of Isla Mujeres, adjacent to Cancun, where rents were much cheaper. They trekked back and forth as foot passengers on the slow car ferry. Jessica had seen the exhausted constables sleeping on the long narrow seats during the forty-minute crossing. For some unknown reason the municipal police worked soul-destroying shifts of twenty-four hours on and then twenty-four hours off, repeated over and over again. No wonder they were occasionally caught napping in a vehicle tucked into a dark corner of the island. It was beyond belief that they could even speak, let alone function, after working twenty-four hours straight.

As they neared her house, a chilly wind brought a light spattering of rain.

"Ah, that feels good," Jessica said, enjoying the rapid drop in temperature. The last three days had been oppressively hot and sticky, like the buildup to a big thunderstorm on a hot summer's day.

"This is the leading edge of the storm," Luis said matter-of-factly. He parked his moto at the curb. "We'd better get inside."

"Will your bike fit through my door?" she asked, eyeing the handlebars and the width of her entrance.

"Yes, but are you sure you want it inside?"

"Certainly," she said, "a little mud on my tile floor won't hurt anything." She unlocked the door, and bent to greet Sparky. "Hi little man. You have to move out of the way, and let Luis in," she said, trusting him to understand everything she said.

She held the door until Luis had the front wheel of the moto inside, then she moved to the back door and opened it. "Come on boy. Last chance for pees and poops." The wind barged through the house, jerking the door out of her hand. "Dammit!" she yelled, scrambling to grab the door with both hands to prevent it from squashing Sparky's back legs.

At the same time the scooter cleared the front door, allowing it to slam loudly, shaking the doorframe. "Sorry, Jess. I didn't have enough hands to stop it," he said ruefully.

"No worries, I shouldn't have opened this one until you were inside. I didn't think it was that strong yet."

"It will build quickly. Better get the pooch back inside as soon as he's finished his business."

Chapter 14

August 28th – 2:00 a.m.

Dark.

Carlos glanced down at the shadowy form huddled against his chest. Between them they might be occupying barely a third of the king-sized bed. The large mattress really was too wide for the room, leaving a narrow passageway on either side to get in and out of the bed, but he enjoyed being able to stretch out and not feel cramped. Except of course when a beautiful woman, a frightened, over-heated beautiful woman, wanted to jam herself as close as possible to his side.

Hot.

He and Yasmin were hot and slick with sweat, and not from having fun in bed. There was just no way to cool down. The electricity to the island had been shut off. No electricity meant no ceiling fans and no air conditioning. His bedroom window was a slider secured by a locked cortina, but with the wind and rain raging outside they didn't dare crack it open for a bit of fresh air.

Loud.

Tormenta Isla

The roar of wind sounded as if they were standing beside a jet when the engines were thundering in preparation for takeoff. The intense wind ominously pulled at his aluminum shutters, shaking them like a terrier with a rat. A parade of what sounded like garbage cans, plastic bottles, and empty plastic buckets bounced along the road and slammed off obstructions including, quite likely, his precious Porsche. A neighbour's sheet metal roof screeched as high-speed gusts picked at a loose edge, like a child worrying a half-healed scab. The glass globe from a street lamp dropped to the pavement with a nerve-jarring explosion. A few minutes later, something else struck the ground with a heavy ground-shaking thud.

Recoiling at the noise, Yasmin dug her fingers into Carlos' back, causing him to wince. "What was that?" she asked.

"It might have been a power pole falling over," Carlos said, kissing the top of her head as he gave her a reassuring squeeze. "The one at the corner was badly cracked and leaning."

"But it's concrete," she protested. "It should be stronger than the old wooden ones."

"It's twelve years old and weakened by corrosion." he said. After Hurricane Wilma in 2005, most of the power poles had been replaced with new concrete ones reinforced with iron rebar. The airborne ocean salt, salitre, leached into the interior through pinholes and hairline cracks. As the iron rebar rusted, it increased in size, pressing against the casing until the structures split open like over-ripe fruit.

It had taken eleven crews of electrical workers three weeks to restore the power on the island after Wilma. Brought in from other cities, the men worked non-stop to install poles, string wires, and replace transformers.

A bright flash of light, followed closely by a thunder clap, shook the house. Carlos sighed, wondering how long the storm was going to last. At least he had been able to talk his mom, dad and Tia Norma into leaving the island before the car ferry had stopped operating. They were now safely tucked away in Valladolid with his brother Roberto and his family. A few less things to worry about.

~

"Crap! That was close!" Jessica exhaled a sharp breath as a flash of lightning and a simultaneous crash of thunder shook the house, immediately followed by two more bright flashes and seemingly instantaneous loud claps of slightly less intensity. Even the candle flame seemed to quaver with the intense noise.

"No kidding," Luis agreed, as he hopped out of bed. "I'll do a quick look for problems." He reached for the flashlight lying on the bedside table, flicked it on and headed to the living area.

Snuggled in her bed, Sparky trembled against her ribs. Her dog was not normally afraid of thunder, but that explosion had been exceptionally close and deafeningly loud. Her ears were still ringing. She lightly rested her chin on the top of his head. "We'll be okay, little man," she whispered, to reassure him.

She sniffed the air. It had an odd odor, similar to the electrical smell that hung around when her microwave had recently caught fire. The ever-present curse of living in a humid and salty environment; electronics and electrical components suffered hugely. Her microwaves generally lasted a year at the most before shooting blue flames out through the fan.

"I smell something odd," Jessica said, gently pushing her dog aside as she swung her feet to the floor. "Be right back, Sparky, you stay here." Which, naturally, he didn't. Where she went, he went. His moist nose nervously bumped against her calves as she walked.

In the kitchen Jessica sniffed electrical outlets, light switches and appliances while Luis inspected the living area and the bathroom. Her small casa crouched between two other modest homes, so the risk of a direct hit was minimal. There was nothing tall in the immediate neighbourhood to attract a lightning strike, and nothing super flammable like wooden roofs or grass palapas. The dangerous, but less obvious hazard, was a fire inside the house, caused by the energy traveling through the electrical and telephone lines. She remembered one hot August afternoon when she and her parents had been enjoying the spectacle of a late summer thunderstorm at their home in Canada. A bolt of lightning had struck the service pole for their house. The excess energy had travelled through the interior wiring and melted the kitchen telephone. She could still remember the stink of burning plastic coming from the smouldering device on her mom's granite counter. Good thing no one had been using it at the time.

A few minutes later she said, "I still smell that weird odor but everything seems okay. What do you think, Luis?"

"Si, I vaguely remember something from high school science classes. Something about electrical arcs splitting oxygen molecules and creating ozone. Ozone stinks like that," he said. "I'm sure we're fine."

He reached inside the refrigerator and removed two bottles of beer, twisted off the caps, and handed one to Jessica.

"Cheers," she said, lightly clinking the neck of her bottle against his, then taking a sip. "Umm. It's still quite cold even though the power has been out for hours."

Tormenta Isla

"Enjoy it while you can," he said. "It could be days, or even weeks, before the electricity is restored."

Chapter 15

August 28th – 2:00 a.m.

The baby, Ana, wailed. "Shhh, mi amor. Shhh. It's okay," Diego whispered to his youngest daughter, his lips lightly grazing her soft cheek. He cuddled her close to his chest, hoping the sound of his heartbeat would calm her, although his was pounding at a double-time speed. Those last thunderclaps had been loud enough to scare the pants off him. José, always trying to be the brave older brother, sat with his shoulder grazing Diego's arm. He refused to be hugged. Yet.

Diego glanced around the room; other than three anxious tear-stained faces, everything seemed to be okay. Cristina's eyes met Diego's. He could see she was frightened, so he flashed a big cheesy grin and winked. He mouthed, "I love you."

Her arms protectively wrapped around Pedro and Luisa, Cristina weakly smiled and whispered, "I love you too, mi amor."

There were two lanterns, one on the kitchen table, and one on the coffee table. Both were battery powered and should last quite a few more hours, plus they had a stockpile of candles as a backup. Cristina had said she didn't want to use the candles unless it was absolutely necessary. She was worried that the little ones would knock them over and cause a fire, or burn their hands.

He sincerely hoped this storm was going to quickly move over the island, but without electricity there was no internet and no way to confirm its status. Hurricane Pablo had arrived shortly after midnight and now, two hours later, they were really feeling the brunt of the high winds. Maybe four or five more hours and it would be gone. If, that is, it behaved in a typical manner and didn't linger over the island like Wilma in 2005. That storm had stalled overhead for almost three days of unrelenting winds, rain, thunder and lightning. He had been single at the time and the fierce tormenta had been an exhilarating experience, but now with a young family to worry about it was a different event altogether.

He silently offered up a prayer to a god that, except for Christmas and Santa Semana, Holy Week, he had all but ignored since his childhood. He hoped someone up there was listening to him.

"Anyone thirsty?" he asked, to distract the younger ones from their tears. He turned to José, carefully handing him a now quieter Ana. "Would you like a Coca, son?" They seldom offered sugar-filled soft drinks to the kids, but sometimes exceptions had to be made, and this was one of those times.

"Si Papi, gracias," José said, snuggling his little sister.

Diego opened the still cool refrigerator and removed a can of Coke, then set it next to José. He turned to his wife. "Cristina, what would you like?"

She mouthed 'wine.'

He smiled, "water? Good choice. I'll get you a nice big glass of water."

Cristina rolled her eyes, watching as he poured a generous slug of white wine into a water glass and set it beside her. He gave her shoulder a reassuring squeeze. She nodded her thanks.

He waggled his eyebrows at Pedro and Luisa, "and what would the Señor and Señorita like to drink this evening?"

"Coca!"

"Right, two colas coming right up," he said, serving the youngsters.

"Now, what should I have?" he said, pulling a comical face and pretending to think very hard. Then he turned to Luisa, "What should Daddy have, honey?"

"Cerveza," she replied, sniffing back her tears. "Papi loves cerveza."

"Very good. Papi does love cerveza." He grinned foolishly at his daughter, then opened a bottle and took a sip. "Ah, the perfect choice," he said, making Luisa giggle as he extended his baby finger in the manner of an English matron sipping a cup of tea.

Diego squeezed himself onto the crowded sofa beside Cristina and the two kids. He put his arm around her shoulders, encompassing Luisa in the hug. "This is very cozy," he said.

Cristina looked at him and laughed, "You big goof. I do love you."

~

The wind hammered against the door, demanding to be let inside. Pedro ran a hand over the wooden door and frame, confirming everything was still secure. He had forgotten how loud the uproar of a hurricane could be – the howling wind, the driving rain, and the frequent lightning flashes followed by ear-splitting thunder claps. He wished he had a set of noise cancelling earphones, the type used by shift workers who had to cope with their unusual sleeping routines.

He turned from examining the door, smiling down at his mom who was perched on the edge of the sofa. The candlelight softening the deep wrinkles on her face, he silently watched her fingers as she whispered a decade of Hail Mary's on her rosary. The string of carved wooden beads had been a gift from her parents on her *quinceaños*, her fifteenth birthday, and the beads were satiny from fifty years of daily devotions. She refused to replace the rosary even though Pedro had recently given her a new one for her sixty-fifth birthday.

She had affectionately thanked him for his gift then carefully placed the beautiful string of amber and silver beads in a velvet box. He had seen her hide the box underneath her *delicados*, as she called them, in her underwear drawer. In her mind the gift was too pretentious to use for her daily prayers, and hiding it under her bras and panties would ensure that it would never be stolen. No thief would dare rifle through a respectable woman's underthings!

As she finished her recitation, Consuela Velazquez looked up at her son and smiled.

"Are you doing okay, mama?" he reached out and tucked her delicate hand into his big brown mitt.

"Si, God will take care of us," she said, giving his hand a light squeeze.

He nodded. He admired her strong conviction, but didn't share her beliefs, although he would never, ever, say that aloud. His mother would be horrified to know her son was a nonbeliever.

Chapter 16

August 28th – 5:25 a.m.

Silence.

Jessica popped opened one eye and listened. The fierce noise had suddenly ended. "Luis, wake up." She reached over and gently jostled his shoulder. "It's over. The storm is gone." She tossed off the top sheet and plopped her feet onto the tile floor. The single sheet, pulled over her hot sticky skin, was not for warmth but to absorb some of her sweat. The house was stifling hot and airless. It would be great to open the doors and let the air flow through.

"Uh-uh. Not over. Just half-way," a sleepy voice mumbled.

"What?" she asked, pulling a t-shirt over her head.

"Give me a minute. My brain is still in neutral," yawning, Luis pulled himself into a semi-sitting position and leaned against the headboard. He scrubbed his face with both hands, then peered at Jessica, "It's the eye of the hurricane."

"Oh, sure, I've heard about that," she said. Damn, he was sexy even when sleep-deprived and half-awake. She picked her shorts off the dresser top and stepped into them. "I'm going to open the doors for fresh air, and let Sparky into the garden for a pee."

"Just open the back door, and only for a few minutes," he said, getting out of the bed and reaching for his pants. "It's still a dangerous situation. Once the eye passes we'll be back into hurricane-force winds and torrential rainstorms."

"Okay. Come on baby. Hurry, hurry," she said, half-running towards the back door. "Come on boy, pees and poops."

Sparky's nails clicked on the tiles as he scurried after her.

She opened the back door and surveyed her new freshwater lake. The water lapped at the stairs of her little patio, and appeared to be deeper than the height of Sparky. "Dammit."

Sparky poked his nose out, sniffing the air before cautiously stepping onto the concrete patio. He glanced up at Jessica. His worried expression and bouncing eyebrows seemed to ask, "are-you-sure-about-this?"

"Quick, have a pee," she said, pointing at a plant container that he annoyingly, although sporadically, marked as his.

Tormenta Isla

"I am," Luis replied, his voice coming from the bathroom.

"Not you, the dog."

~

Yasmin was awake; she hadn't slept a wink since the storm's arrival. Stretched out beside her, one arm tucked behind his head, Carlos was quietly watching her.

"The eye," she said.

He nodded, "si, the storm is moving quickly. It should be past us in a few more hours."

"So far so good," she said, then quickly sketched the sign of the cross.

He smiled at her reflexive movements. She had once told him it was a habit, learned from her grandmother, as protection from evil spirits who might decide to punish her for a rash comment, for her impudence.

"So far, very good," he agreed. "Since we are awake, would you like a cup of coffee?" he asked, rolling over and getting out of bed. "I'm going to make a fresh pot."

"How?" she asked. "The electricity is off." He could hear the light taunt in her voice, as if he had forgotten that they didn't have power.

"Gas stove. You know that black thing in the kitchen that doesn't require electricity to work?" He said. "You should try using it sometime."

"I cook," she retorted, "just not often."

"Uh huh, sure you do." He pulled on his black boxer shorts, embroidered with two white pineapples and the word 'Cool.'

"Sexy shorts. Where did you get those?"

He leaned over and kissed her lips, "a beautiful woman with gorgeous green eyes bought them for me. I think she wants my body," he murmured.

"Yes, I think she does."

He could feel her warm skin tremble as he nibbled her earlobe. He kissed her, letting his tongue gently explore her mouth, then reluctantly straightened up and padded barefoot towards the kitchen. "Still just milk, no sugar?"

"Si, gracias mi amor."

"Anything for a beautiful woman who lusts after me."

Carlos hand-pumped the purified water from a twenty-liter plastic jug, a garrafón, into a saucepan. Then he reached under the counter and flipped a lever on the propane line to the open position. The twenty-litre tank was located outside the house and had a standard valve closure. He didn't like the valve being open all the time, but he couldn't be bothered to go outside to turn it off every time he was finished cooking. As a compromise he had installed a second shutoff under the stove. A few clicks of the barbeque lighter and he set the pan on the metal grid.

He enjoyed coffee made with his expensive Italian espresso machine that sputtered hot steam and made all the required noises that to a connoisseur said exceptional coffee was being created. But without electricity they would have to make due with hot water slowly poured into a filter basket, balanced over a small saucepan. Not ideal, but caffeine was one of his dietary requirements. Luckily, stashed in his freezer was a supply of recently ground, dark French-roast coffee. His emergency supply.

While he waited for the water to boil, he wandered around the house, checking for problems. There was a small lake by the front door where the fierce wind had shoved the rain around and under his makeshift sandbags. All of the windows were leaking. It was a common problem with concrete houses; the window frames just never seemed to be completely watertight. Before the storm, he and Yasmin had laid old towels and rags along the sills and near the entrances. In between pouring more water over his make-shift coffee filter, he gathered up the wet towels and wrung them over the kitchen sink. The towels would have to be replaced, and the entranceway needed mopping, but everything would have to wait until he had fresh caffeine running through his veins.

So far the house was holding up just fine. He hoped everyone else was doing okay. Not every islander was fortunate enough to afford a sturdy house like his.

Dozens of people lived in windowless structures made of a loose combination of concrete blocks and bits of wood, topped with tin or palapa roofs. Hopefully they had all been able to find room at the civil defence shelter in the centre of the island. It was a large empty warehouse-type structure that provided protection from the rain and wind, but not much else. He had offered space in his home to a few of the old-timers, the seniors without a lot of resources. Most had said they were moving in with family; a few said they had already made arrangements with friends.

"Did you go to Starbucks for my coffee?" a plaintive voice asked.

"Coming *princesa*," he said, pulling two large pottery mugs from the shelf and filling them with the dark liquid and a touch of milk.

Chapter 17

August 28th – sunrise

Edgar Valdez cursed as he shifted uncomfortably in his wet hammock. Yesterday he had decided against going to the civil defense shelter. He had an instinctive aversion to police, firefighters, or other city officials who would be overseeing the influx of islanders. It was best to keep a low profile.

In the tightly packed colonia of Guadalupana the dwellings were crammed into miniscule lots that did not have, until very recently, the basic services of electricity and running water. The Invasion, as it was derisively named by other islanders, was the brain-child of a long ago municipal politician. The man had confiscated a piece of property for non-payment of land taxes, divided it into tiny parcels, and sold the pieces to locals who had dreams of owning property instead of renting. Then he moved to another country. More than ten years later the purchasers were still trying to obtain a legal title for their small piece of paradise. Valdez didn't care one way or the other about the legality of anything. His only concern was self-preservation.

Tormenta Isla

He glanced upwards. The roof had leaked badly during the night, and water was still trickling into his insubstantial dwelling through a dozen or more rips in the grass thatching. The shack that he lived in belonged to another man, and as part of the cheap monthly rent Valdez was responsible for any repairs. He couldn't fix the palapa until the storm had moved on. The eye had just passed over and he could feel the wind from the opposing eye-wall pressing against the wood and tin shanty.

He scrubbed his whiskered face with a calloused palm. Unlike his Mayan acquaintances who had very little facial hair, he had inherited his whiskers from a European ancestor somewhere far back in the family tree. His dead mother, may she rot in Hell, said their genealogy was more like a shrub than a tree. Trees had long branches. Shrubs were compact. She was referring to the second-cousin-to-second-cousin marriages prevalent in the tiny village where he was born, south of the American border and north of nothing.

He tossed aside the wet blanket, and stumbled into the small space that pretended to be a bathroom. The corroded shower head dripped rusty water into a bowl-shaped concrete drain. A tiny sink with one functioning faucet clung precariously by two rusted bolts to one wall. The deeply stained toilet had no seat. He unzipped and took a leak while staring at the spider-webbed wall just inches from his face.

Hungry, wet and miserable; the high life of a cartel foot soldier. Working for Rafael Fernandez, a Cancun kingpin, was supposed to be the easy route to riches. But not for him. He was forty-seven and living in a shack. He scraped out a living by building palapas, the favourite covering for a beach restaurant, or as a quaint feature on the expensive houses built by foreigners. It was hard and, depending on the height of the structure, often dangerous work. He occasionally made a bit of extra cash by selling his small allotment of drugs to other workers or by cleaning up a mess for Don Rafael. Stupid men, like the taxi driver Ricardo Villarreal, thought they could get away with cheating the drug lord. They invariably met an abrupt and bitter end.

Scratching his unwashed armpits, Edgar sauntered to the mini-fridge that he had rescued from the island's scrap metal dealer. It was dirty and badly dented, but when he had electricity, it functioned well enough to keep his beer cool. He pulled out two lukewarm bottles. Twisting off the cap, he downed the contents of the first bottle in five swallows, then burped long and loudly. He tossed the bottle into a corner where it jangled against other discards. The second bottle he took back to his wet nest in the hammock.

Tormenta Isla

Ah, the breakfast of champions. Maybe the beer would help him sleep through the second half of the storm that was beginning to pummel his flimsy home once again.

~

The fierce winds resumed beating against the walls and battering at the doors of the civil defense shelter. The wail of an unhappy child echoed through the building, followed by a second and a third, each child's fear feeding off the others. Constable Alexis Gomez sat on the floor, her shoulders pressed against the wall. She and her partner, Sergeant Filipe Ramirez, plus two other police constables, had been assigned to maintain an orderly atmosphere inside the building.

Alexis stared across the sea of people crouching, sitting, or laying on the concrete floor. A few had hung hammocks from the wall hooks, others had brought blankets and pillows or huddled inside thick jackets. Many of the youngsters leaned into a parent or an older sibling as they dozed fitfully.

Perched at the highest point of the island, the building was crowded with hundreds of islanders who exhibited everything from abject fear to calculated indifference. She longingly thought of her snug home, her comfortable bed, and a bathroom that wasn't awash in the bodily fluids of strangers. Scared people developed diarrhea, nervous stomachs, and weak bladders. The stench of the close-to-overflowing toilets was nauseating.

She and the other cops were at the end of their regular twenty-four hour shift. Everyone was exhausted, but they couldn't leave until their captain had given the okay to open the doors. Even then, it was likely they would be needed as traffic control for the flooded streets, or be required help the injured. It was going to be a long, long time before she could put her head down and sleep, really sleep.

"*Con permiso.*" Filipe stepped over a dozing man and slid his long frame down the wall to settle beside her. "Gracias," he said politely to another woman as she shifted slightly to give him a sliver of space. He smiled at Alexis, and tiredly winked. The corner of her lips tipped up in a half-smile.

"How are you doing?" she asked, tilting her gaze up to meet his.

"Surviving," he said.

"Si," she nodded in agreement, "I've been fantasizing about my bed."

He bent his head lower and whispered, "Me too, with you in it."

She dug an elbow into his ribs. "Shhh." Her dimples deepened with suppressed laughter.

"Naked."

Tormenta Isla

She shot a worried glance past Filipe. The woman sitting beside him seemed to be ignoring them, so perhaps she hadn't heard his lewd comments. "Filipe, behave," Alexis murmured.

He just smiled and carefully stood up. "Carry on constable," he said, tossing her a salute. She watched him carefully pick a route between the people, as he headed back to the other side of the building.

People were becoming restless with their confinement, and Alexis' eyes roamed over the crowd looking for potential problems. She made eye contact with the woman beside her but couldn't quite read the expression on her face. Did the woman feel Filipe's lustful comments to his subordinate had been inappropriate? Or did she realize they were lovers and was amused?

Relaxing her shoulders against the wall, Alexis blinked her eyes closed for what felt like a millisecond. Her head drooped, bobbing twice before she jerked herself awake. Pushing off the floor with one hand, she regained her feet. She had to move or she was going fall asleep where she sat. That would be an inspiring sight, a police constable open-mouthed and drooling. Everyone had a phone camera these days and an incriminating photo plus a sarcastic comment could be quickly posted on social media. Well, it could be posted when the internet service was restored. If that happened she would be called into the captain's office and lectured about falling sleep on the job, and a notation would be placed in her employee file.

She sighed deeply. She had been inside this building for nearly eight hours. She and the other police officers had arrived before the storm to ensure everyone that needed shelter was inside and the doors secured.

When, when, when was this going to be over?

Chapter 18

August 28th – noon

Carlos lifted his head from the pillow and listened. Silence filled the house. They had fallen asleep again, exhausted by the inescapable noise and the sheer boredom of waiting for the storm to end. He reached out and gently stroked Yasmin's shoulder.

"Carina, wake up."

"Umm? What?"

"I think it's over." He kissed her cheek, then moved to get out of the bed. "I'll look." He quickly pulled on a pair of shorts and a t-shirt, padding barefoot into the living area.

"Cuidado, mi amor," she said, warning him to be careful.

"Si, of course." It was impossible to see through the boarded up windows, so he laid his ear on the wooden door. "It's pretty quiet out there. I'm going to look." He released the lock, then braced himself as he eased the door open. The wind had died.

"Is it over?"

"I think so," he said, fully opening the door and staring out to the street. "Ah hell!"

Yasmin heard the sadness in his voice. She quickly dressed and hurried towards him. "What's wrong?"

He flicked one finger, pointing at the street.

"Oh no. Your car," she said, pushing past him to get a better look.

"Wait," he said, pointing at the debris in the street, "put something on your feet."

Yasmin pulled on her sandals, stepping cautiously through the drifts of loose paper, broken glass, plastic bottles, and palm fronds as they inched their way forward, stopping where the water lapped at the sidewalk's edge. She stared open-mouthed at the squashed remains of the black Porsche. It was pinned under a concrete utility pole, undoubtedly the same one that had shaken the house when it fell.

"Oh, Carlos."

"It's just a car," he said, trying to appear nonchalant, pretending he wasn't shattered by the loss of his expensive toy. His baby. "Let's hope that's the worst that happened."

He lifted his gaze from the wreckage and studied the street. A number of power poles were down. Others were tilted at gravity-defying angles. The telephone, internet and power lines were on the ground, all tangled like cooked noodles that had been tinted black with squid ink. A few curious neighbours opened doors and poked their noses out, like cats cautiously sniffing the air before exploring an unfamiliar location. Carlos lifted an arm and waved. As if an all-clear signal had been broadcast, more doors opened and people ventured out onto the street.

Rudy Garcia sloshed through the water, crossing from his side of the street to stare at the Porsche. "Shee-it. It's totalled."

Dressed in his customary sleeveless t-shirt that displayed his tattooed biceps, the man stood feet braced apart with his burly arms crossed over his chest. His favourite t-shirt style was scornfully referred to as a wifebeater shirt, presumably because men who wore those shirts were the lowlifes that beat their wives. In Carlos' experience, clothes had nothing at all to do with which man would or wouldn't abuse his wife and children. Even some of the most well-dressed, respected citizens were known for blackening their wife's eyes, and their children were frequent visitors to the emergency clinics. He had absolutely no patience with men who battered their families, and believed they should all be left to rot in jail. On the other hand, he knew from firsthand experience that Rudy Garcia was a good-natured teddy bear who adored his plump wife and three rambunctious kids.

"Si," Carlos nodded. "A bit too much for you to fix this time, hermano," Carlos grinned ruefully at his neighbour. Rudy was a competent repairman who worked out of a small work shop in the back of his house.

"You have insurance?"

"Yes, but you know how those bastards like to drag their feet."

Rudy nodded agreement, then leaned forward trying to peer into the flattened sports car. The heavy cross and thick chain that he habitually wore around his neck swung forward and rapped against what had been the passenger's door. "Lo siento," he said, apologizing as he tucked the icon inside his shirt.

Carlos just snorted a laugh, "another scratch isn't going to matter one damn bit."

~

Valdez lifted his head from his wet pillow, smacked his dry lips and let loose with a long and satisfying fart. He had a raging thirst and his stomach grumbled noisily. He couldn't remember the last time he had eaten, certainly well before the storm arrived. He glanced up at the sky centred over his hammock, looking through what had been a palapa roof. Not much remained of the structure, except a few supports and a couple of small areas of thatch.

Searching for his phone, he was surprized to discover that it still lit up despite being wet. He checked the device; no signal. He tried to call Don Rafael. Nothing. No service, and no electricity. He turned the phone off, no sense wasting the battery life.

Reluctantly he uncurled his stiff muscles and put his feet on the wet floor. He shuffled towards the toilet and unzipped, splashing piss on the rim of the toilet and the floor. He'd have to get the cleaning lady to take care of that, he mused. Maybe she could make his bed, wash his clothes and cook a meal too, if he had a cleaning lady.

He wondered how he was going to earn a living while the municipality got back on its feet. He would eventually get work but everything depended on the depth of the damage to the community. If the car ferry was operational supplies could be brought over. If not, that would be another big delay. If the roads were destroyed, or buildings collapsed, there would be more delays.

His side business of selling recreational drugs was going to be very slow until the tourists returned to the island. *Sept-hambre*, the month that was traditionally the slowest time of year with the lowest amount of income available for islanders, might take on a whole new meaning this year. Starting today there were going to be a lot of hungry people looking for work, any type of work, to feed themselves and their families.

He needed to talk to Don Rafael. Maybe he would have another job for him. Money was money. It didn't matter to him how he earned it. Even beating Villarreal's stupid wife until she told him where to find the drugs that her thieving, but already dead, husband had hidden hadn't bothered him. He had then graphically explained what would happen to her teenage daughter and young son should she decide to go to the police for help.

Chapter 19

August 28th - noon

Jessica cocked her head, listening. Yep. No wind. "Luis, do you think the storm is over this time?"

He nodded, "It sounds like it. Let's look."

They had been lounging on the bed, alternating between dozing and fitfully flipping through old magazines as a means to pass the time. He cautiously unlocked the back door, and stepped onto her patio. The yard was still knee-deep in water, but now that the rain had stopped, it would start to drain. "Looks good, let's see what's happening on the other side."

Jessica opened the front door, and yelped, "Oh my God."

"What? What's wrong?" Luis leaned against her back, peering over her shoulder. All he could see was a swift river of water flowing where the street should be. It covered the road from side to side as it rushed towards the lower elevations.

"It's a dog. I'm not sure if it is dead or alive," she said, moving slightly so that Luis could see where she was pointing.

Sparky poked his head through her legs and sniffed. The pile of fur stirred slightly.

"Be careful Sparky," Jessica said, "it might be alive." She was still uncertain if she had seen the creature move, or if the wind had rumpled its wet fur. Sparky pushed past and ran his nose along the inert form. His tail fanned back and forth a couple of times.

A low moan escaped from the wet heap.

She turned and pointed into her bedroom, "Luis, get me the blanket from my bed."

Luis stared at her for a long moment. He looked as if he was going to refuse, then he shrugged a shoulder and did as she asked. She turned her attention back to the animal.

"Here, Jess," he said, handing her the blanket and a pair of thick work gloves that he had seen in her kitchen drawer. "At least put these gloves on, in case it bites you."

"Good idea. Now, can you open the door to my spare room, I need to put him, or her, somewhere safe until I can get it to a vet."

Again Luis gave her that look, the one that said she was certifiably crazy, but he knew she wasn't going to change her mind anytime soon.

"Sure," he said.

She gingerly stepped over the form, speaking softly as she moved. "Hey buddy, you're going to be okay now. Don't worry." With no idea what had happened to the animal she was reluctant to move it, in case she made the injuries worse, but she knew the two veterinarian clinics would soon be swamped with emergencies, so she had to at least try to help it in the interim. "Luis, can you tell this guy in Spanish it's going to be okay?"

"What?"

"Just talk softly, say nice things," she said, letting her eyes slide quickly past Luis' face, not making eye contact. She knew his expression would be one of astonished disbelief, and she might laugh. Now was not the time to indulge in her off-beat sense of humour.

"Okay."

Listening to him mumble in Spanish to the dog, she slowly squatted down and let her hands settle on the animal. The gloves made it impossible to feel anything so she removed them and set them aside. She glanced at Luis' worried glare. "I'll use them later when I move him."

"Him?"

"Just guessing," she said, as she gently palpated the areas she could reach; a leg, then another, then the ribcage, feeling for broken bones and cuts. "Yep, definitely a male, with all the bits attached."

The animal moaned again but didn't pull away from her probing fingers. She carefully felt the skull and got a look at its small black floppy ears, narrow dark muzzle and golden fear-filled eyes. "Shhh. Todo bien. Todo bien."

Sparky moved so that the other dog could see him, his tail waving in his let's-be-friends mode. He didn't crowd the other animal, he just stood close and looked friendly.

"I have to move him to finish checking for injuries, so I might as well carry him inside at the same time," she said.

"I'll do it," Luis offered, moving towards her.

"No, it's okay. He's skin and bones. I can pick him up." She carefully draped the blanket over the dog, then ignoring the thick gloves, slid her hands under his scrawny frame and gently curled him into her arms. He screamed with pain and flipped his head back to stare at her, but he didn't try to bite her. "Easy boy. Almost there," she whispered as she walked through the living area, past Luis' moto that they had stashed inside the night before. She carried the pooch into her miniscule guest bedroom-storage area.

Luis flattened the blanket as she carefully lowered the animal to the floor. Then she started a second assessment of injuries.

Tormenta Isla

He was covered in dozens of engorged ticks, including deep inside his ears. No surprize there. It was the norm on the island unless an animal was medicated on a regular schedule.

The dog howled when she felt along his hips and spine. "Likely hit by a car." She turned to look at Luis. He was crouched beside her, watching what she was doing.

"I don't imagine anyone was driving last night," he said.

"True. Then maybe he was hiding under something and it collapsed on him."

"That's more likely," Luis agreed.

"He doesn't seem to be bleeding but without x-rays I have no way of knowing if he has internal injuries," she said, picking up her phone to call Dr. Delfino. "Damn it, no service."

"Without electricity nothing works."

"I have to get him to the clinic."

"We only have my moto," he reminded her.

"Diego. He has a Jeep."

"Again, no electricity, no phone."

"Would you drive to his house and ask him if we could borrow his Jeep?"

Luis sighed melodramatically then leaned towards her, and nibbled her bottom lip before kissing her. "The things I do for love," he said, getting to his feet and putting on his jacket.

They wrestled the moto out of the house and back onto the street. Luis waved, then cautiously drove along the sidewalks, avoiding the deepest water.

"Wait a minute," Jessica called after his receding form, "You said love. You said, 'the things you do for love.'"

Chapter 20

August 28th - early afternoon

Luis pulled up in front of Diego and Cristina's, and gratefully dismounted from the moto. The ride from Jessica's had taken three times longer than normal. He had dodged around flooded streets and rode on sidewalks when there was no other route available. He had skirted downed trees, broken utility poles, and shattered glass, plus the bodies of several cats and dogs that had been left to fend for themselves. There was nothing pretty about the aftermath of a hurricane.

He knocked on the front door, "Diego. Are you home?"

"Si, si, *momentito*," came the muffled reply.

Luis heard what sounded like nails being pulled out of wood and then the door opened. "You nailed your doors shut?" he asked.

Diego looked over his shoulder, then whispered, "Cristina was certain the wind would blow the doors open. It was the only way I could get her to calm down."

"Oh, sure," Luis said, thinking he wouldn't want to be inside a house with the doors nailed shut. That would feel too much like being inside a coffin after the undertakers had screwed the lid closed.

"I opened the back door first so the kids could get outside, but their play area is still under water," Diego said, then asked, "How did you get here? Aren't the roads flooded?"

"The intersections and lower roads are submerged, but I managed to find a route through on my moto."

"Is it bad?"

"It's pretty ugly out here," Luis said, "you might want to keep the little ones in the house as much as possible."

"Good idea. Did you need something or are you just checking on us?"

"Both actually," Luis admitted. "I wanted to make sure you are all okay, and I would like to borrow your Jeep for an hour or two."

"Sure, what's up?"

Embarrassed, Luis didn't answer.

"Luis, why do you need my Jeep?"

"Jessica wants to take a dog to the veterinarian."

"Sparky? Did the little guy get hurt?"

"No, not Sparky. Another dog."

"Ah, you're kidding me. She wants to put a bleeding, dirty, tick-infested dog in my nice clean ride."

"It's not bleeding," Luis replied.

"Oh, well that's okay then. It's just a dirty and tick-infested mutt, but it's not bleeding."

"She's got it wrapped in a big blanket."

Shaking his head, Diego murmured, "Jessica, Jessica, Jessica." He reached into his pocket and held the keys out to Luis, then said, "She owes me for this. Big time."

Luis just nodded, and handed his moto keys to Diego. "In case you want to use it."

"Great. Two useless motos." Diego grumbled.

~

Back at Jessica's house, Luis parked the Jeep in the middle of the street. He turned on the four-way flashers and shut off the engine. He hopped from the cab and landed on the sidewalk, which was now visible under the slowly receding water.

Opening her front door he hollered, "Hi honey, I'm home," imitating a television comedy character.

"Five minutes."

He could hear the toilet flush and water running in the sink then the bathroom door opened.

"Any problems?" she asked, as she dried her hands on a small orange towel.

"The streets are a mess, but we should be okay. What are you going to do if the clinic isn't open?"

Luis was relieved. Jessica was concentrating on the injured dog and seemed to have forgotten his flippant quip about the things you do for love. As soon as he had made the remark, he had regretted it. In truth he wasn't exactly sure how he felt about her. Liked her? Absolutely. Loved her? It was too soon to know for sure.

She huffed out a breath and shrugged. "No clue. Let's go see." She tossed the towel onto the bathroom counter and walked towards the guest bedroom. She knelt to scoop the dog into her arms.

"I wish you would let me do that for you," Luis said, holding the front door open.

"He doesn't weigh much, and he trusts me." She glanced down at Sparky who was following at her heels. "Okay bud, you can go with us. Maybe that will keep this guy calmer."

Luis opened the back door of the Jeep, stepping back while she laid the blanket-wrapped dog on the seat. Sparky hopped in and carefully sat beside the injured mutt, his feet tracking water and mud from the street onto the light grey fabric.

"Diego's going to love that," Luis muttered.

"What did you say?" Jessica asked as she climbed into the passenger seat and closed the door.

"The mud on the back seat, Diego will be thrilled," Luis said, as he started the vehicle and checked his mirrors. He turned off the flashers and eased forward.

She turned to look, "I'll clean it up before we return the Jeep to Diego."

Luis stopped at the intersection, glancing both directions. "No traffic," he said. The drive into the northern end of the colonias where the Clinica Veterinaria was located was a tedious repetition of his earlier journey. His biggest concern was puncturing the tires on unseen hazards, the bits of twisted metal, glass, or who knew what else that was hidden in the water of the flooded streets.

"What a mess!" Jessica said, gazing at the destruction around her.

He nodded. "No serious damage to houses that I can see. The taller hotels and condos in Centro might be a different story though."

Chapter 21

August 28th - afternoon

Luis stopped Diego's Jeep as close as possible to the front doors of the Clinica Veterinaria on Jesus Martinez Ross Avenue. The large front window was boarded over with pieces of plywood, but the painted aluminum door appeared to be slightly ajar.

Jessica was already opening the Jeep's door before he had the vehicle in park. "Wait here and I'll check to see if either of the doctors are here," she said.

Jammed in one corner of the entrance patio was a jumbled pile of black plastic crates, the kind the Chedraui grocery store managers gladly gave away whenever possible. Fresh vegetables, arriving on the island twice a week, were shipped in the heavy, moulded-plastic boxes from the wholesalers. There was no recycling plan for the bulky containers, but a few were repurposed to other jobs, like pet beds, dog-carriers for motos, or household storage bins. Many just ended up in the garbage dump.

Water dripped slowly from the sopping collection of bedding inside the plastic containers. This area was normally the domain of the street cats that snoozed in the shade and waited for food. The staff wouldn't have left the animals to fend for themselves during the hurricane. The neutered toms and tabbies would have been tucked in with the other eighty-odd cats and six dogs that lived in the sanctuary behind the clinic. In their rush to secure the felines they had likely left behind the pile of make-shift beds. Miraculously they hadn't blown or floated away.

She pulled on the metal handle and peeked into the gloom, "Anyone here?"

"Si," answered a male voice. "Come in, come in." He shone a flashlight on the floor to show her the way.

Jessica pulled the door open all the way. Empty! No one was waiting. "Hola Doctor Delfino. I am so glad you are here."

"Hola Jessica, everything is okay with you?" he asked, twisting the English a little with his Spanish cadence. A mass of long, dark, and curly hair peeked out from under his surgical cap.

"I'm fine, thank you. I'm really surprized your waiting area isn't stuffed with injured pets."

"Soon, it will take a little time for people to get mobile," Delfino said with a worried smile on his face. "Then it will be a very busy time for the staff and me. How can we help you?"

"I have an injured dog. Can you look at him?"

"Si, si. Come in, please." He waved her forward.

Holding her thumb and forefinger separated by a small space, she said, "*momentito*, a moment please," and walked to Luis who was leaning against the back fender.

"We're good to go. I'll take the pooch inside." She gingerly scooped the dog into her arms and headed towards the clinic. She heard Luis lock the vehicle, and then heard his and Sparky's footsteps following behind her. Luis reached ahead and held the door fully open as she stepped inside.

"Dark," Luis commented, "and hot."

"Very." she agreed.

An hour later Jessica and Luis exited the clinic without the dog. Under the beam of three flashlights held by Jessica, Luis and a technician, the veterinarian treated the pooch for a broken leg. The dog would stay two or three nights just to ensure everything was okay. While he was sedated, he had been cleaned, neutered, groomed, and treated for parasites. He was already looking very different from the moaning, filthy mess that she had discovered on her front doorstep just a few hours ago.

"What are you going to call this one?" Luis asked.

"I'm only keeping him until we find his owners," she said, avoiding his knowing smile.

"Uh-huh. Sure you are."

"Can we check on Carlos and Yasmin before we take Diego's Jeep back?" Jessica asked as she opened the rear door for Sparky. "Come on, in you go, boy."

"I'm not a boy," Luis retorted. "I'm a mucho macho hombre."

Jessica rolled her eyes, "I was talking to Sparky."

Chapter 22

August 28th – early afternoon

Pedro carefully picked his way through the ankle-deep water and rubble as he walked the short distance towards Cristina and Diego's house. His parents had insisted that he check on their daughter and the grandbabies. They trusted Diego to care for them but they wanted reassurance that everyone was okay.

The front door was open and he shouted a greeting.

Cristina appeared from the kitchen with baby Ana balanced on a hip. She stood on tiptoes to kiss her brother's cheek. "Todo bien?" she asked. "Everything okay with mama and papa?"

"Si, si. They sent me to check on you," he said, pointing at his wet feet. "Do you have a rag or something I can dry my sandals on?"

She flapped a dismissive hand, "Don't worry. Come in. The floors are muddy from the kids wading in the backyard. They keep running into the house to use the toilet, or get a drink of water, or just make a nuisance of themselves," she said, smiling.

"Okay, thanks. Everything okay with you, sis?"

"Si, we are fine. Just tired." She bounced the baby on her hip. "We were a little scared, but we're okay now," she said, wiping a bit of drool from Ana's mouth.

"Where's Diego? I don't see his Jeep outside." He reached his arms out, indicating that he would like to hold his young niece.

"Jessica has my Jeep," a deep voice rumbled in complaint from the kitchen.

Pedro's eyebrows shot up and he mouthed, "Jessica?" to his sister. He bounced Ana in his arms a few times, kissing her chubby cheeks.

Cristiana stifled a grin and nodded.

Pedro wasn't sure who she was laughing at; Diego for being cranky because Jessica had borrowed his Jeep, or at him for the baby drool on his face. He wiped his face and dried his hand on his pants, then sauntered into the kitchen with his niece in his arms. Pedro shifted the baby to one arm and pulled a kitchen chair away from the table. He sat down and balanced her on one knee, then jiggled the leg up and down.

"Jessica has your Jeep," he stated, rather than asked.

"Si," Diego grumbled. "Luis said she needed to take a dog to the clinic. An injured mutt, not Sparky."

The crinkles in the corner of Pedro's eyes deepened as he fought off a laugh. He knew Diego babied his vehicle but he would never say 'no' to Jessica. There was a tight friendship between the two, nothing romantic, more like a big-brother and a pain-in-the-butt younger sister relationship. "That's Jess, always willing to help an injured animal," he pointed out, bouncing his knee harder to make Ana giggle.

"I know, but it's my Jeep!" Diego protested, glaring at Pedro.

Turning the conversation to a less touchy subject, Pedro asked, "Have you see Carlos yet?"

"No, have you?"

Pedro shook his head, "but, I am going to drive over to his house after I report back to mom that everything is fine here." He cocked a smile at his sister. They knew their mother would not relax until she knew everyone in the family was okay.

"Let us know how he is doing. I only have our moto and Luis' moto for getting around, and I imagine the streets are still flooded."

"Si, especially in the lower areas. There is still a lot of water draining from the higher levels." Pedro stood up and replaced the chair right way around. Then he bussed his sister's cheek one more time with a light kiss, and smooched the top of baby Ana's head as he handed her back to her mother. "Okay, I have to go or Mama will send a search party out to find me."

"Pedro?"

"What?" he asked, his hand on the front door handle.

"After you see Carlos, come back and get me. We should check on the boat."

"Si."

~

Pedro parked his truck near Carlos' house then whistled long and low when he spotted the crushed Porsche. "Nasty." He hopped out of the vehicle, avoiding the flooded street and landing on the drier sidewalk.

The front door to Carlos' house was also open. Like everyone else they were trying to cool the house with fresh air. "Carlos?" Pedro shouted through the entrance.

"Si?" came the reply, as Carlos appeared in the doorway.

Pedro pointed, "bad news about your wheels."

Carlos shrugged, but a look of sadness flashed across his face. "It's just a car."

Yasmin came outside to join them, hugging Pedro briefly then standing beside Carlos as they silently surveyed the wreckage.

Catching the hint that his buddy didn't want to discuss the mangled mess that had been his pride and joy, Pedro asked, "everything else okay?"

"I don't know." Carlos," he said, pointing at the Porsche. "No wheels. Would it be possible for you to give us a ride to my parents' house so that I can have a quick look?"

"Sure."

"*Momentito*, I'll get the keys."

"I'll come with you." said," said Yasmin as she turned to follow Carlos inside. "Just let me get my purse and phone."

"Your phone?"

"For photographs, for insurance claims."

"Right. Good idea." Back outside, Carlos stood on the edge of the curb with his hands shoved in his pockets. He sadly studied his car. "Can you take a few pictures of the Porsche before we go?"

"Of course," Yasmin said, activating the camera app on her phone.

"I think I see Diego's Jeep headed this way," Pedro said, pointing to the approaching white vehicle.

"I guess he's come to check on us too." Carlos replied.

"I don't think so. I was just at his house. Jessica and Luis have his Jeep."

Carlos turned to look at Pedro, "Why would Jessica borrow Diego's Jeep?"

Pedro smiled, and said, "It's a long story that involves an injured dog."

Carlos nodded, and said, "Claro, Jessica and animals. No need to explain any further."

Luis stopped the Jeep and set the brake, then turned off the engine. He stepped out of the cab, "Good to see you are all okay," he said, greeting the guys with fist-bumps and a kiss for Yasmin.

"Hey everyone," Jessica shouted cheerily as she and Sparky joined the group.

The next twenty minutes passed quickly as they discussed the storm and then planned what they should do next. Carlos was very anxious to see what had happened in Centro and to check on his restaurant. The Loco Lobo was street level, with only a mesh security grill that was pulled across the open area at closing time. The restaurant was wide open to the wind, rain, and flooding.

Yasmin said she would keep him company, to give him moral support and to help out where she could. Jessica was anxious to search for islanders who needed assistance.

She decided to keep Sparky with her instead of delaying everyone by trying to take him home.

Luis said he wasn't overly concerned about his office. He had good solid storm shutters and all of his important files had been moved to his second floor mezzanine. He promised to return Diego's Jeep, and he also wanted to stop at the home of his cousins to make sure everyone there was okay.

Settled inside the Nissan, Carlos asked Pedro, "Would it be possible to get a ride to the Loco Lobo after we have a quick look at my parent's place?"

Pedro scrubbed a hand over his bald head as he considered the request, "I was planning to go back for Diego so we could inspect our boat," he said, then hollered out of the window, "Luis! Tell Diego I will be a bit delayed. Can you help him check our boat?"

Luis gave him a thumbs up and nodded.

Chapter 23

August 28th – afternoon

Valdez rummaged in his ruined dwelling like a stray dog searching for scraps in the municipal dump. He was looking for a bit of food, dry clothes, or a jacket. Anything to ease his discomfort.

Opening the top drawer of his wobbly three-drawer dresser, he yanked out his spare pair of pants. "Shit. Shit. Shit," he yelled, angrily tossing the sodden jeans onto his filthy floor.

Stomping around in the constricted space, he cursed loudly, not caring what his neighbours in the tightly packed settlement thought. They typically avoided contact with him anyway, glancing down or finding something fascinating to look at on their phones whenever he was nearby. It suited him just fine.

Valdez reached down, picked up the pants and tossed them over the back of his one chair. He'd just have to wear the clothes he had on, eventually they would dry out. In the meantime he needed food, and more beer.

Tormenta Isla

He cautiously poked his head out of his entrance, half expecting a damaged palm tree or a piece of someone's metal roof to whack him on the head. The fierce winds and rain had stopped and he could now hear the ocean waves once again. They sounded much larger and closer than normal.

He indifferently surveyed the cramped colonia where he lived. The driving rain and fierce winds had badly damaged dozens of the insubstantial dwellings. The few homes that actually had glass windows before the storm didn't have them now; snaggletoothed shards poked from window frames. Several doors were askew, and roofs had been peeled off like wrappings torn from a parcel. Many shanties, like his, didn't have a proper door, only an open entranceway. The torrential downpour had gouged a waterway across the dirt floors as the water raced downhill towards the ocean. Normally the colonia was a tolerable place to live, located across the street from the eye-catching turquoise Caribbean Sea, but now it resembled a landfill, a garbage dump. He wasn't the only one facing uncomfortable nights for the foreseeable future. Not that he cared one damn bit about anyone but himself. He agreed with Don Rafael's outlook on life, survival of the meanest.

He walked around his battered grey truck. It looked about the same, perhaps a few more scratches and small dents but all four tires were fine and the headlights were intact.

Tormenta Isla

He pulled open the driver's door and hopped in. He started the truck, and it kicked to life on the first try. Well that was something at least.

~

Sea water, pushed by the ferocious winds of Hurricane Pablo, invaded the Salina Chica. The deep water scoured the abused basin, scrubbing out decades of trash, dead creatures, and a large, plastic-wrapped, odorous bundle. Pushed forward with the wind and the current of the rising water, the bundle bumped across the airport in rhythm with the waves.

Once a valuable commodity for the islanders, this salina was now the forgotten landlocked pool, hidden by matted vegetation at the end of the seldom-used airport. Five hundred years ago, when the Spanish discovered Isla Mujeres, the islanders were already using salt as a preservative for fish and turtle meat. The villagers of Delores, the Spanish name for the settlement at the northern tip of the island, collected salt at the beginning of each fishing season.

In an atmosphere of a family outing, adults and children would trek barefoot over the rough pathway through the tangled undergrowth to one of the three salt pans, Salina Grande, Salina Chica, or Salina del Cañotal. Salt gathering was hard physical work, especially for the women. They would stand waist-deep in the briny water, scooping the salt into turtle shells, then carrying it to the shore. After drying the salt in the sunlight, it had to be back-packed to the community. Later the men would traverse the ocean with canoes laden with salt and dried fish to trade for deer meat, treasured jade and obsidian, warm cotton blankets, and delicious Yucatan honey. They traded as far north as Veracruz and south to the present day Puerto Morelos.

The salt pans were in use as late as the early 1970s, when the availability of electricity and then refrigerators on the island made preserving fish and turtle meat with salt redundant.

Now the salinas were just a place to toss unwanted garbage.

Chapter 24

August 28th – afternoon

"This is terrible," Yasmin whispered.

"No kidding," Pedro said.

He leaned forward, propping his forearms on the steering wheel, surveying the area ahead. He had stopped the truck on the small incline just before the gas station on the eastern side of the island. The low lying area of Aeropuerto Road, north of the Bachilleres high school and across from the PeMex station, was flooded. It looked to be at least thigh-deep, judging by the water lapping against the walls of the building.

"Look at all that junk." Jessica said, pointing at a raft of debris swirling in the murky water. She was in the back seat of the four-door pickup with Sparky balanced on her lap. His back feet were planted on her thighs and his front feet resting on the window ledge. He pushed his snout out the window sniffing deeply. His shiny black nose twitched rapidly, taking in the different smells.

Palm branches, outdoor furniture that hadn't been properly secured, palapas that had recently shaded secluded patios, dead iguanas, dead fish, anything that would float, spun around and around in wide lazy circles resembling a giant sink drain. Pedro slowly moved the Nissan forward, expecting at any moment to feel the road drop from under the front wheels as they were sucked into the swirling vortex.

Carlos said, "This was the same area where Hurricane Gilbert cut a channel right across the island in 1988. We were just kids. Remember that Pedro?"

"Si, I do. Our families lived in Centro where the grocery stores and freight boats were located. We had a better chance of getting food and clean water when it arrived on the island," Pedro said, remembering the scarcity of fresh food after the hurricane. "Some of our school friends and their families were cut off longer, stuck on the other side of the channel."

"Remember how we felt sorry for them because they lived out in the sticks, the untamed part of the island," Carlos said.

"Si."

"No one died of starvation, but lots of people were hungry. Especially the ones who couldn't afford to buy food," Pedro said.

"What did they eat?" Yasmin asked. "I was too young to remember."

"Fish, turtle meat, turtle eggs, iguanas. Whatever they could find," Pedro shrugged.

Jessica made a face of distaste. "That sounds disgusting." Sparky wagged his tail in apparent agreement.

Carlos shrugged, then nodded towards the substantial houses lining both sides of the road. "All the utility lines have been destroyed and most of the poles are broken off, but the houses look okay, at least from this side. They might have water damage on the ocean side."

"I hope everyone is okay," said Yasmin.

"This area is mostly gringo owners who live here in the winter months. I doubt any of the houses are occupied," Pedro said, as he slowly crept his vehicle forward.

"Except Punta Piedra," Yasmin said, pointing towards the long collection of white buildings on the beach side of the road. "They're locals who were also here when Wilma hit in 2005."

"There are at least three other couples that live in this neighbourhood year-around; two are Americans, one is Canadian." Jessica said. "I've chatted with them at the restaurant a few times. They all seem pretty level-headed and capable enough to ride out a hurricane."

"I think the high school is okay, too," Yasmin said, cranking her head around to look over her shoulder at the one-story all concrete structure on the land side of the road. It was built without windows to allow the breeze to fan the stiflingly hot classrooms. It would be filled with mud and plant debris, but it looked intact.

"A friend of mine is the vice-principal of the school," Pedro said. "She told me the computer lab is the only room with glass in the windows. The staff removed the electronic equipment and boarded the windows. Structurally it should be okay, but it will be filthy inside."

Pedro put his foot on the brake, staring at the deep water.

"We might have to abandon this idea for now," Carlos said. "You don't want to destroy your truck just so I can look at my restaurant."

"If the water is this deep here, Centro will be completely flooded too," Yasmin said.

"Yeah," Carlos nodded glumly. "I can only imagine the mess. The hurricane-force winds will have pushed the water right over the seawall, the malécon, and into the colonia. I am pretty sure everything at street level will be flooded; homes, shops and restaurants.

Pedro nodded, "Okay, let's try again tomorrow morning. Maybe the storm surge will have calmed down by then, and the road will be passable."

Yasmin handed her phone to Carlos, "can you take a photograph so I can show the others?"

"Sure," he held the phone out the window and clicked a couple of pictures, then handed the device back. "I really wish we had some way of finding out what's going on in Centro."

"Maybe we can ask them," Jessica pointed at an orange and grey rigid-inflatable Zodiac coming towards them. The captain was cautiously maneuvering the craft through the debris.

Carlos opened the passenger door of the Nissan and stood up, keeping his feet inside the cab of the truck. He leaned his weight on the top of the door frame and waved his arm at the three marinas. "Hola!"

His hands cupped around his mouth to project his voice, the Navy officer shouted, "Turn back. You can't go any further."

"Si, claro, but what's happening in Centro?"

"It's badly flooded. The roads are not passable."

"Can we help in any way?"

The man shook his head. "Not right now. Give your names to the police or the Red Cross. We want to know everyone is safe."

Carlos shouted back, "I have a small boat." He fumbled in his pocket and pulled out the metal fob with his father's keys attached, including the one for the boat's ignition. "We could help search the houses for people who need assistance."

The Navy officer held up a hand signalling him to wait a minute, then keyed the microphone on his radio. He talked, then listened, then spoke again. He nodded at something the other person said, then stowed the radio. "Okay, but we don't have room for everyone in our boat."

Pedro turned to Yasmin and Jessica, "I'll go with Carlos. You two can take my truck and leave it at his house."

The captain nosed the boat closer, allowing the men to step from the inside of the vehicle into the boat.

Jessica tucked Sparky under her arm, and hopped across uninvited.

"Wait! Señora, no dogs."

"He's a registered Search and Rescue dog," she said.

Pedro cocked an eyebrow at her, and grinned. *Registered Search and Rescue dog – and pigs might fly.*

Chapter 25

August 28th – late afternoon

"Unbelievable." Carlos murmured, casting an eye over the waist-deep water.

On the bayside of the street, beach front restaurants were awash. Their waterfront docks that were normally busy with arriving and departing tour boats were underwater. On the land side of the double-wide avenue, the debris-filled seawater lapped at the imposing perimeter walls of the Navy base. The large metal security gates, a black grid of welded iron bars, were adequate protection against human intruders, but allowed the storm surge to invade the parade area and the ground floor of the building.

"It is odd to be boating down the middle of Rueda Medina," the officer agreed. He had introduced himself as Captain Valentino Dzul, then popped one shoulder up in a half-embarrassed dismissive gesture and said, "my mother's choice. Just call me Tino, and these guys are Jose Luis and Gabriel," he said, nodding towards his crewmen.

"Mucho gusto," Carlos said, shaking hands briefly with everyone. "I'm Carlos, this is

Pedro, Jessica, and Sparky." he said, pointing as he informally introduced the group.

"Mucho gusto," the marinas replied in response.

Captain Dzul eyed Sparky, "Registered Search and Rescue dog?" he queried.

"Yes, and he's famous for capturing an escaped killer."

Dzul looked at the dog again then nodded, "Claro. *Chispito*, Sparky. The dog who also uncovered the buried pirate treasure."

"Exactly," Jessica said.

Carlos could see the hint of amusement in the Captain's face. He would accept the dog in his boat, as long as Sparky behaved himself. At the moment, the pooch was happy to stand on a seat with his paws on the side of the inflatable, his long ears flapping in the wind, and his sensitive nose investigating every new smell.

Unable to contain his curiosity any longer about the fate of his restaurant, Carlos asked, "Have you been on Hidalgo Avenue yet?"

"No, not yet. Why?"

"I own a restaurant, the Loco Lobo. I'm anxious to see how it fared."

The captain glanced at Carlos and nodded, "Of course, Carlos Mendoza." He turned the steering wheel to the right, piloting the watercraft along Abasolo Avenue towards Hidalgo. "Okay, let's see how close we can get for a quick look. Then if you are serious about helping us search, we will need to get life vests and flashlights for everyone."

"We are willing to help in any way possible. Any chance of a handheld radio?"

"I'll see what I can do." the captain said. "In the meantime everyone keep your eyes open for problems." The water level dropped the nearer the boat came to the centre of the colonia. The propeller briefly nicked the paving stones, and Tino quickly put the two Yamaha motors in neutral and powered the motor legs into the up position, giving the boat more clearance.

Carlos and Pedro strained their necks to the left, trying to see as far as the Loco Lobo. Jessica's eyes flicked up and down, checking buildings for any indication that someone needed assistance.

"I can wade over to the entrance," Carlos said. He put one hand on the edge, preparing to swing his leg over the side.

"Wait," Tino gestured for Carlos to stop, "we have paddles." He indicated the two long wooden oars that were secured along the inside of the boat.

The two enlisted men, Jose Luis and Gabriel, unlatched the clasps and slipped the paddles into the water. They guided the craft north towards the intersection of Hidalgo and Matamoras.

Carlos pointed, "Here," and the men stopped. "Humph," he sighed, staring at the muck, sand, coral bits, trash, and a brightly coloured, but very dead, parrot fish on the upper level of the restaurant. A number of the beautiful photographs, taken by his good friend Tony Garcia, had marks across the middle of the images showing how deep the water had been at the worst point. The metal security gate was bent as if something heavy had hit it, but when he reached out from the boat and gave it a firm shake, it felt solid. He craned to look at the tables and chairs still stacked and tied together at the back of the restaurant.

"It doesn't look bad, Carlos," Jessica said, "filthy, but you know we'll all pitch in and clean it up. Structurally it looks okay."

"Si, you're right," Carlos agreed, "my biggest problem will be the refrigerators, dishwasher, and walk-in-coolers. The motors will likely be ruined by the salt water." He turned to Tino. "Is it possible to get us around to the side entrance, just to make sure it is still secure?" he asked.

"Claro," Tino nodded at his two crewmen, who pulled on the oars and propelled the Zodiac closer to the intersection.

Again Carlos was able to reach out and yank on the metal gate, confirming everything was still locked up tight. "Okay, thanks, Tino. There's nothing I can do here right now, so how can we help you?"

~

Exhausted, Sergeant Ramirez slumped behind the steering wheel of his police cruiser parked beside the emergency shelter. A few hours ago the all-clear had been given to allow the doors to be opened and for people to leave the building.

Located on the highest point of the island, away from the flooding on the lower levels, he didn't yet have a clear idea of the situation. His radio had died an hour ago. It needed a recharge, but unless by some miracle they had a generator at the police station, that wasn't going to happen. Hopefully the Captain had a backup supply of fresh batteries, otherwise policing the island without radios was going to be hopeless. At least the wind and rain had stopped, and by tomorrow the sky would be a brilliant blue, the departing gift of a hurricane.

He smiled at his partner Alexis. Her mouth was slightly open as she snored softly, crumpled against the passenger door. She would be embarrassed if he mentioned it, but knowing how they like to rib each other, he probably would – after they were both well rested. Teasing a tired and cranky she-bear never ended well.

Tormenta Isla

They had been on duty now for over thirty-six hours and he didn't give a good god-damn if anyone saw her sleeping. Once she had grabbed an hour or two, he might do the same, assuming they weren't called to deal with an emergency before then.

People milled around, uncertainly. Some of the motos parked outside the shelter had been damaged by flying debris, or knocked over by the wind. A few had flat tires. He imagined the individuals were deciding if they should return to their homes, or if they should wait and sleep another night inside the shelter. Many would likely find their insubstantial dwellings flooded, flattened, or roofless. He only hoped that the small home he shared with Alexis had been spared.

The good thing was, as municipal cops their meager wages would continue, unlike most of the islanders in tourism-related jobs who would have little or no income while the island recovered. Petty crime, especially theft, was going to increase dramatically. Tempers would flare, and battery of wives and children would be more prevalent. People were going to be hungry and scared, and then angry as time dragged on and the politicians dithered.

Ramirez scrubbed at his face with two hands. He needed sleep, at least ten hours, or if not sleep then food and lots of strong coffee.

Chapter 26

August 28th – late afternoon

Diego paced, five long strides to the back door and five long strides to the front door. Where the hell was Luis with his Jeep? And where was Pedro?

"Mi amor," Cristina said, "please sit down, or get out of my way. I'm trying to make a meal for everyone."

His head jerked towards her, "What?" he distractedly asked.

She pointed at a chair. "Sit, or go away and let me cook."

"I want to know what's happening out there. I can't stand not knowing."

"I know, me too. But you are driving me crazy," she said, "You've been obsessing about the Jeep since Luis drove away. Relax. He'll bring it back." She used the back of her hand to push a rebellious piece of hair higher on her forehead, away from her face.

"Pedro said he would come back and get me so that we can check the boat for damage," Diego said, hearing a tone in his voice that sounded suspiciously similar to his youngest son whining about an imagined injustice.

"Perhaps he's helping someone else."

"Humph," Diego said, dropping his mass onto a kitchen chair, causing the wood to groan in protest with the sudden weight. Then, hearing a vehicle stopping outside, he leapt out of his seat, striding for the front door. He charged through the entrance, nearly knocking Yasmin off her feet.

"Yasmin!" he said, grabbing her upper arms to steady her. "I'm sorry. I thought it was Luis returning my Jeep."

"No worries, I'm okay." she laughed.

He peered around her shoulder, "Why are you driving Pedro's truck?"

"He, Carlos, Jessica, and Sparky are helping the marinas search in Centro for people who might need help."

"Is it bad there?"

"Diego, for heavens' sake, let her come inside the house," Cristina called out.

"Perdón, please, come in Yassy." he said, stepping back and motioning her to enter.

"Thank you," she said, "we were only able to drive as far as the Bachilleres School. Then the sailors arrived in a Zodiac and said we couldn't go any further."

"Did the officer have any information?"

"He only said Centro was flooded by water too deep to drive through."

"I should be helping."

"I brought the truck back because Pedro said you wanted to inspect the boat."

"Si, si, I do. Thank you," he said, then added, "but where is Luis with my Jeep?"

"He said he would return it to you, then stop by his cousin's. Maybe he stopped there first," she said. "He should be back soon."

"Diego, go check on the boat," Cristina said. "I will feed the children and save some for you."

Diego cast a quizzical glance at his wife, "Are you trying to get me out of the house?"

Cristina rolled her eyes, "Yes, I want you out from under my feet for a few minutes." She smiled at Yasmin. "Please stay and eat with us. We have plenty to share."

"Thank you Tina, but I'd like to go with Diego," Yasmin said, "I really want to see what's happened to our community."

Diego pulled his head back and looked as if he was going to object when Cristina cut in, "Diego, take her with you." she ordered.

"Okay," he said, meekly. "Let's go, Yasmin." He held out his hand for the ignition keys.

Yasmin tightened her fist over the keys and shook her head. "I'll drive," she said, heading towards the vehicle.

Diego huffed unhappily, then gave Cristina a quick kiss. "I'll try to be as quick as possible, mi amor."

"Be safe and bring Yasmin back for a hot meal." she said, "Now go, shoo."

~

Yasmin started the motor, put the vehicle in gear, and smoothly accelerated away from the curb. The street was still awash in ankle-deep water as the overflow from side streets and yards rushed towards the ocean.

"Are you sure you want to drive?" Diego asked.

Yasmin slanted a wry look at him, "I have been driving since I was a teenager and I haven't killed anyone yet, but there's always a first time."

"It's not far. I could just walk to the marina."

Yasmin laughed, "Diego, are you worried because I'm driving?"

"I'm not a good passenger," he admitted, as they bounced through a hidden pothole. His hand curled over the passenger's armrest, squeezing until his knuckles were white.

"What you mean is you are not a good passenger when a woman is driving," she said. "It's only a short distance. You'll survive." Then she stopped the vehicle at the intersection of Rueda Medina and Calle Fragata and looked in both directions. "No traffic."

"I saw a police truck cruise our neighbourhood a few hours ago, but that's all I've seen," he said. "There won't be a lot of traffic until the streets dry up. Almost everyone uses motos or golf carts to get around, and they stall in deep water."

Rueda Medina, was flooded from sidewalk to sidewalk. The water splashed halfway up the truck's tires. The utility lines were draped over trees and buildings in jumbles, as if a giant kid had gone wild with a can of Silly String.

"Was it like this on the eastern side of the island?" he asked, pointing at the wires.

"Yes, but it was worse along Aeropuerto where there are still a few empty lots."

"Why would that make a difference?"

"Without an oceanfront house to block the wind, the utility poles took the brunt of the force, and snapped in two." She spun the steering wheel, turning the vehicle north towards the marina where *La Bruja* was berthed. "The part I hate is being cut off from everyone. We have no clue if anyone needs help, or if anyone died. It's awful not knowing."

"I agree. It could be days or even weeks before the utility companies can fully restore the electricity and the internet."

Yasmin slowed the vehicle where she knew there was a particularly harsh tope, the inescapable Mexican speed bump, hidden by the deep dirty water. "We can't just drive around all day looking for friends. Eventually the vehicles will run out of gas."

Diego nodded, "I have a few of the sixty-litre plastic carboys of gas stashed in our outdoor shed. But you're right, without electricity we can't easily get more fuel from the gas stations." He said. "Although after Hurricane Wilma some of the boat owners set up a temporary business of ferrying containers of fuel from the mainland to Isla."

"But, we don't even know if Cancun is still operational," she said.

"Stop here. This is the entrance." Diego said, pointing to the tall wooden gates lying flat on the ground. "Or was." he corrected.

Yasmin maneuvered the truck across the road and parked under the sad remains of a *flamboyan* tree. The beautiful lacy leaves and brilliant orange blossoms had been scoured from the branches, leaving a collection of bare sticks and broken limbs.

She slid out of the vehicle, carefully placing her feet on the sodden ground. She was wearing a pair of plastic flip-flops, a very poor choice of footwear for the conditions, but she didn't own anything other than sandals or stilettos. It might be time to buy something like tennis shoes, those bulky, unsexy, but serviceable shoes, or maybe a pair of rubber boots. Bright yellow rubber boots. She would look like a skinny, oversized duck, but at least her feet would be dry.

Chapter 27

August 28th – late afternoon

Diego's feet splashed along the wharf decking as he headed towards *La Bruja del Mar*. The hurricane-strength winds had driven the ocean ahead of the storm, increasing the depth and submerging the fixed-height docks with seawater. The decking was not designed to raise and drop with the tides as was the tradition in temperate zones where the tide differential was greater, changing up to three meters in a twelve hour period. Here, closer to the equator, a normal tide swing was less than one meter, and the dock surfaces were stationary.

The tethered boats thumped against the edge, their fenders floating ineffectually on top of the wharf. Their gel coats, the once shiny outer skins, were scuffed and scratched. One had a deep gash a short distance above the water line and it was almost certainly taking on water. Diego snapped a photo of the name of the boat and the damage. He wasn't sure, but he thought it belonged to Apache Martinez. If he ran into him he would pass along the information, but right now, he had his own boat to worry about.

Not normally a superstitious person, he had his two fingers crossed on his right hand and silently prayed for a bit of luck. Stern-tied to the wharf, and cross-tied to other boats, *La Bruja* wobbled in her berth in rhythm to the rise and fall of the waves. "Damn, I hope she's okay," he muttered.

"Who me?" asked Yasmin, with a hint of sarcasm in her voice.

"Oh hell, sorry Yassy. I forgot you were behind me," Diego said as he glanced over his shoulder.

"No worries. I insisted on coming with you." She held her flip-flops in one hand as she carefully picked her way barefoot along the flooded docks. The water was calf deep on her slim legs. "How's *La Bruja*?"

"Don't know yet, but she seems to be listing a bit to port."

"Sure, listing to port," Yasmin said, leveling her gaze at him.

"I meant she's leaning a bit to the left."

"Oh good, you can speak in a language I understand."

"I'm going to the bilge to see if she is leaking."

"The bilge, another foreign word, which means...?"

"The bottom of the boat, but inside where all the mechanical stuff is hidden."

"Bottom of the boat and mechanical stuff. Now that I understand," she said. "What can I do to help?"

"Just stay here while I look for leaks in the hull." He tapped his knuckles against the fiberglass exterior. "This is the hull in case you don't recognize that word either."

Yasmin laughed.

"Seriously though, stay here in case I get into trouble," Diego said.

"Si, of course." Her dark green eyes reflected her anxiety.

Diego unlatched the entrance gate in the handrail and stepped on board. He crossed the back deck to the main door and stuck his key in the lock. Sliding the door to the right, he stuck his nose inside. He took a deep sniff, searching for the smell of a propane or gas leak. Everything appeared to be okay so he waved at Yasmin and stepped inside.

Wet. Everything was wet. He reached down and squeezed the settee cushions. Wet, but not sopping wet, so maybe caused by rain water leaking in through windows and not flooding. The carpet underfoot squished out water with his footsteps but still not as serious as it could be. He continued on to check the forward stateroom and guest quarters. All okay except for the dampness. He and Pedro would have to come back and open up everything to let it dry out. Ideally, placing fans throughout the boat would be the best solution but without electricity, sunshine and fresh air was the only remedy. He then opened the door to the head, or if he was speaking to Yasmin, the bathroom. Everything seemed ship-shape, no leaks.

He retraced his steps to the back deck, and once again waved at Yasmin to let her know everything was fine. "I'm going into the bilge," he said, pointing at the large access hatches on the back deck. He unlatched the locks, lifted the heavy covers to the vertical position, and clambered down the short ladder.

Water. But how bad was it? He listened. The bilge pumps weren't working. The batteries had been fully charged, so the pumps should have come on when the water had accumulated in the hull. The wires had likely shorted out.

~

"Is this the boat?" the captain, Tino Dzul, asked. He pointed at a *panga* that was floating in a wide, horseshoe-shaped courtyard. It was tethered to the set of stairs leading to the second floor of the house.

"Si, that's my pa's boat. He's in Valladolid, and I have his keys." Carlos said.

"Strange place to leave it."

"Not really, it's my auntie's house. Dad normally beaches the boat across the street near Restaurante Velázquez. He stashes it here when we are expecting a violent storm."

Tino nodded. "We should check on your aunt while we are here."

"No need, she went to Valladolid with my parents a few days ago," Carlos said, letting his eyes roam over the exterior of the building. "The house looks secure. I'll come back once the water recedes."

"Where are the motors?" Tino asked.

"Inside that bodega," Pedro said, pointing to a half-submerged hut inside the walled enclosure.

"Do you need help putting them back on the boat?" Tino asked, looking meaningfully at his younger crewmembers.

Realizing Dzul was offering his two subordinates as workhorses, Carlos laughed. "No we're good, thanks Tino," he said, watching the relief play across the younger men's faces. Each motor weighed a bit more than a grown man and it was a gut-wrenching job mounting them on the stern of the boat. "Pedro and I have done this dozens of times."

"Oh yeah, and it is such a fun job," Pedro said, as he steadied himself on the edge of the rigid-inflatable. He waited until the captain had cautiously pushed past the floating debris and snugged the two boats together, then he crawled into the fiberglass fishing boat. It was calf-deep in rain water, but still floating. "We've got a bit of bailing to do," he said.

"No bilge pump?" Asked Tino.

"No," Carlos said, pulling himself into the *panga*, "not worth the constant hassle with the rust, corrosion, and petty theft. Dad replaced a few over the years and finally gave up." He held up two plastic pails, "These buckets and our arms are the bilge pumps."

Jessica piped up, "I'll bail while you two get the motors setup." She shifted into the *panga*, and then turned to lift Sparky but he easily jumped the gap. "Good boy."

She stretched her arms to take the flashlights, three life vests and the handheld radio from Gabriel, the youngest of the crewmen. "Is the radio set to your frequency?" she asked.

"All set," replied Gabriel, "just keep it on that channel."

Tino said, "If you're sure you don't need our help we'll head out and continue searching for folks who need assistance."

Carlos gave him the thumbs up, the Mexican version of okay. Many a tourist learned to their dismay that the conventional sign language for okay, a thumb and finger formed into a circle with the other fingers splayed behind didn't mean okay – it meant *pendejo*. Asshole. It amused his restaurant staff when they asked a customer, "How was your meal this evening?" and the smiling customer would happily flash the asshole signal.

Pedro waved, "We're fine, thanks Tino. We'll let you know as soon as we are mobile."

Jessica waved goodbye to Dzul. Cute. Too bad she was already hooked on Luis.

Chapter 28

August 28th – early evening

"We need a megaphone to let people know we're here," Jessica said. "The water is too deep for people to leave their homes, and the windows are covered so we can't see if someone needs help."

She wrinkled her nose. The normal fresh salty smell of the ocean breeze was tinged with the smell of death. Dead creatures – fish, crabs, iguanas, cats, and two dogs sloshed in the waist-deep water. As the water receded the smell would intensify until the carcasses could be gathered up and buried, or be eaten by scavengers like other crabs and birds. The thought was disheartening, not something to be mentioned in tourist advertisements.

Carlos said, "Pedro, try yelling."

Pedro cupped his hands around his mouth and shouted, "Hola! Anyone there?" he waited a couple of minutes and tried again, "Anyone need help?"

Jessica held up a hand, "Wait, I think I hear something."

Carlos flicked the gearshift lever into neutral and listened. "I can't hear anything. Can you Pedro?"

"Maybe," Pedro replied. "I thought I heard someone answer back."

"Try again," Jessica watched Sparky's face. His ears were perked up and his tail was straight as he concentrated on a two-storey building. It was a combination of a tienda, a small store, on the ground floor, where the proprietors sold cold drinks, frozen treats, and packaged snacks. The living quarters would on the second level.

"Hola!" Pedro said, putting more volume into his voice, "anyone there?"

"Si," came a muffled response, "up here."

"There!" Jessica pointed at the building that Sparky was studying.

"Do you need help?"

"Si."

"We'll be right there," Pedro shouted, then pointed at the side entrance and said, "Can you get me closer, Carlos?"

Carlos nodded and snugged the *panga* against the building. Pedro stepped over the side and trudged up the stairs. Sparky jumped and swam through the water that, for him, was chest-deep. He pulled himself out of the water onto a dry step, shook himself, and hurried after Pedro.

"Wait for me!" Jessica said, slinging her leg over the side to join Pedro and her dog.

At the top of the stairs, Pedro knocked on the door, "How can we help you?"

"My door is stuck," said an older feminine voice.

Pedro twisted the knob and pushed his shoulder against the door. It wouldn't budge. "Stand back." he yelled," he shouted.

"Claro."

Once again he twisted the knob, then with his big foot battered the wooden door. It popped open, causing Pedro to do a quick two-step to regain his balance.

"Are you okay, Señora?" Jessica asked, entering the apartment with Sparky hot on her heels.

"Yes, much better now." A diminutive woman, who appeared to be in her late seventies or early eighties, fanned her face with a piece of paper and smiled at Jessica. "It was getting very hot inside, and I couldn't unstick my door. I thought I would be stuck in here forever."

"The streets are flooded and you can't go anywhere, *Abuela*," Pedro responded politely, addressing her as grandmother, even though she was a stranger.

"Oh no, I won't. Thank you both again."

"Are you sure you will be okay now?" Jessica asked, glancing around the tiny apartment. "Do you have water and food?"

"Yes, thank you dear. I am fine." the woman said. "Is this your cute little doggy?" she asked, bending over to pat Sparky's head.

"Yes, this is Sparky, or *Chispito* in Spanish."

"He's a lovely little boy," she said, then straightened up and smiled at Jessica, "thank you. I'm fine now."

"What about your neighbours?" Pedro asked.

"Everyone left yesterday. They are staying with family."

"Why didn't you leave before the hurricane, Señora?" Jessica asked.

Jessica could hear the pride in the old woman's voice, "This is my home. I never leave."

A few minutes later, Pedro thumped down the stairs and grabbed the side of the boat, holding it steady while Jessica lifted a very wet dog onboard then hopped in herself. "You probably overheard," he said to Carlos, "her door was stuck. We poked our heads inside and everything else looks okay."

"Good thing we heard her," Jessica said, "It was damn hot inside that apartment."

"Si," Pedro agreed, "the rain has swollen the wood. It will dry out in a day or two."

"But is she safe with a door that she can't close or lock?"

Pedro nodded. "No one would hurt an old grandmother."

"We can check on her again, tomorrow," Carlos replied.

"Good idea."

"Okay. Where should we go next?" Jessica asked.

"I guess we should just keep looking for people who need help. I don't see any major structural damage, just hundreds of shattered windows in the bigger hotels and condo complexes." said," said Carlos.

Jessica could see shards of glass glinting in the setting sun. "I can't begin to imagine how much glass we will find once the water has receded."

"It looks like the buildings that were too tall to board up took the worst of the punishment," Pedro said. "Some have *cortinas*, some don't."

Tormenta Isla

Carlos slowly piloted the boat along Lopez Mateos, the avenue that ran from the northern end of Rueda Medina, in front of the Privileges Aluxes hotel and past the old cemetery, where a lot of the tombs were inundated with ocean water. Most of the graves were ancient, but a few were more recent additions to an ancestral plot. If the occupants escaped and floated away, it would be a gruesome task for the municipal workers to round up the loose bones and the newer decomposing corpses.

"I wonder if Mundaca's tomb is okay," Jessica mused.

"Okay ... as in still empty?" Pedro asked.

Jessica smiled at his reference to the night about a year ago when she and Yasmin had the not-so-bright idea to raid the pirate's crypt looking for his rumoured treasure. His remains were actually buried in Merida. Oddly, he had commissioned the Isla tomb to be built before he died.

"I meant okay, as in not damaged," she retorted.

Pedro chuckled.

"Everything seems quiet along here," Carlos said.

"Quiet as a graveyard," Pedro quipped.

"That joke stinks, even for your odd sense of humor," Carlos said with a shake of his head.

A large grey helicopter neared the island, coming from the direction of Cancun. The impressive machine thudded loudly overhead as the pilot skimmed the coastline of Playa Norte, then turned south. "One of the Navy helicopters, the Blackhawk," Pedro said, his eyes wistfully following the machine making the racket. "I'd love to have a ride in that bad boy."

"I imagine they are temporarily stationed at the Cancun sub-base. There's nowhere for it to take off and land with this airport under water," Carlos said, then added, "Jess, ask Tino where he wants us to look next."

Jessica nodded and keyed the microphone, "Mobile five to mobile three. Come in," she said, remembering the proper radio etiquette that she had learned from her father, a Canadian firefighter.

"This is mobile three. Go ahead, mobile five," answered one of the younger crewmen, possibly the one named Gabriel.

"Roger, mobile three. All clear to the intersection of Lopez Mateos and Hidalgo. Where should we go next?"

There was a slight pause as the sailor asked his boss. "Mobile five, proceed south on Rueda Medina, past the car ferry docks. Check the neighbourhood near the Escuela Técnica Secundaria, the middle school."

"Roger. Out."

"Okay, let's see how close we can get to that area."

Carlos turned the *panga* around, heading back to Rueda Medina and then south to the airport runway.

A few minutes later Sparky's nose was twitching double-time, then he started to whine. Jessica rested her hand on his back. "Easy boy," she said, then added, "Carlos, head that way," pointing in the direction of the car ferry terminal. "I think I see what he is interested in. There's something large bumping against the fence."

"It's just a big bundle of plastic," said Carlos.

Pedro shook his head, "No, Jessica's right. I think we should take a better look. Sparky's unhappy about something."

Carlos pointed the *panga* towards the form. "I hate to say this but it is about the right size for a body," he said, as Sparky's whine changed to a deep growl.

"Oh, god, smell that!" Jessica said, quickly covering her nose and mouth. "Something or someone died."

"It's too big for a dog, and besides, no one is going to wrap an animal in plastic." said," said Pedro.

"Better call Captain Dzul," Carlos said, "I'll pull back a bit, keep us upwind from the smell."

"Stay," Jessica said, then lifted her hand from Sparky's back. She picked up the radio and keyed the microphone. "Captain Dzul this is mobile five, come in please." Sparky remained obediently beside her. His front paws were planted on the gunwales of the *panga*, his eyes focused on the drifting package.

"This is Dzul, mobile five."

Jessica glanced at the odoriferous bundle, "We are near the entrance to the car ferry on Rueda Medina. We think we have discovered a corpse."

"Drowning?"

"Negative, Captain," she replied, "suspicious circumstances."

"Roger that. I'll dispatch someone to investigate," Dzul responded. "Teniente Zapata did you copy that last transmission?"

"Affirmative Captain. Car ferry terminal. Suspicious circumstances," a feminine voice responded. "We are on our way."

Chapter 29

August 28th – evening

As the Navy inflatable neared, Pedro could see two people. One was a woman, dressed in camouflage utilities, with a rifle strap slung across her chest. The gun hung muzzle down, over her back. The other was a young fresh-faced crewman.

"Whoa," Pedro said, "look at that chica. She's packing a big gun. A really big gun."

"Steady there boy," Carlos said, flashing a wide grin.

When the two-person inflatable pulled alongside, Pedro reached out to grasp the side, holding the boats together. Sparky turned to briefly acknowledge the two new-comers, then resumed his surveillance of the smelly package.

"Well, hello there." Pedro's eyes did a quick inventory of the woman. It was difficult to tell in the deepening darkness, but she appeared to have a fit, athletic form hidden under the bulky camo gear, a chest-pack covered with pockets, straps and buckles, thick-soled lace-up boots, and a helmet. He had never met a gun-toting female naval officer before. Sexy in a strange way.

"I'm Teniente Zapata, Lieutenant Zapata. And this is Crewman 1st Class Santiago Alverez. What's the situation?" she asked. Her cool gaze settled on Pedro's face.

"Smooth, real smooth. Jackass," whispered Carlos.

"Maricruz," Jessica said, "is that you buried under all that gear?" she asked.

"Hola Jess. Nice to see you, although not under these circumstances," she replied. To Carlos, the woman's voice sounded warmer and inviting as she answered Jessica.

"We think Sparky has located a cadaver," Jessica pointed at the black object floating in the murky water.

"It appears to be securely wrapped in heavy plastic, and I am quite sure he or she didn't do that voluntarily," Pedro said, trying to lighten the mood with his off-beat humour. He let the flashlight illuminate a neutral space between them, giving enough light so he could see her face but not shining it directly on her.

She regarded him with a neutral gaze. "Right. I see," she responded, then turned towards Carlos. "As you heard on the mobile unit, my captain would like my crewman and me to confirm it is a body. If it is then we will take the cadaver to the naval base."

Pedro could feel his face heat up as he realized that twice in the last few minutes he had put his foot in his mouth, blathering inappropriate nonsense to a competent naval officer. He was oddly drawn to this taciturn woman, wondering how he could get her to return his smile. Her large brown eyes were set in a thin face, her dark hair tightly pulled back and hidden under the helmet. She shifted the rifle in what looked to be a familiar gesture until it was settled under her right arm. Tough woman.

"Do you think this might be the missing taxi driver?" asked Carlos.

"Perhaps," she said, "but we won't know until the doctor or the coroner does the autopsy." She studied Carlos for a moment and smiled, "I recognize you. You're Carlos Mendoza from the Loco Lobo."

Pedro's heartbeat did a double-tap. She had a gorgeous smile that lit up her face, but it wasn't aimed at him. Dammit.

"Do you frequently come to my restaurant?" Carlos asked. "I don't recognize you in your uniform."

"I sometimes pop in for a meal and a visit with Jessica," she laughed lightly as she waved a hand down the length of her frame, "and no, you wouldn't recognize me. I wear girlie civvies when I am off duty."

Tormenta Isla

"She definitely doesn't look like that when she comes to visit," Jessica agreed with a laugh. "She cleans up real good."

Carlos chuckled.

Pedro remained quiet. He knew he had gotten off to a bad start with the woman.

"How are you going to get the corpse back to the Navy base?" asked Jessica.

"We will tow it with our dinghy," Maricruz said, indicating the inflatable. In the beam of her flashlight, the younger sailor looked decidedly queasy.

"There are five of us, why don't we lift it onboard my boat and I will follow you back," Carlos suggested.

Zapata considered the offer for a moment, then nodded. "Okay, thank you. Let's pull alongside," she said, tapping her gearshift into forward and moving slowly ahead.

Madre de Dios!" Pedro muttered, as Carlos positioned the *panga* close to the corpse. His stomach roiled at the stench of rotting flesh.

"It is better to breath with your mouth open," Zapata said.

Pedro blinked in surprize at her no-nonsense tone.

Zapata shucked the rifle from her shoulder, propping it against the seat of the inflatable. She dropped into the water, indicating to her subordinate that he should do the same.

The young marina reluctantly joined his lieutenant, preparing to lift as Carlos and Pedro would begin to pull the odoriferous package onboard the boat.

"On three," Zapata said, "uno, dos, tres." The bundle cleared the water and teetered on the edge of the *panga*, then slithered eel-like into the bottom of the boat.

A stream of liquid ooze struck Santiago in the face. He turned sideways, spewing vomit across the water.

Pedro swallowed hard, concentrating on not puking up his guts. He refused to embarrass himself in front of Zapata. He noticed that Jessica had conveniently taken over handling the boat, letting the guys do the dirty work – for once. She would normally be front and centre of any messy situation. He'd have to rib her about that later, displaying her softer girlie-side. Even Sparky seemed content to sniff from a distance.

The lieutenant calmly hoisted herself into the dinghy, then extended an arm to her young crewman, Alverez. He shook his head and pulled himself onboard, a little less gracefully than she had. She started the motor and led the way towards the naval base just a short distance away.

~

The tall black gates at the southern end of the naval base were wide open, allowing the shallow-draft search and rescue vessels to scuttle in and out when required. A sailor was stationed in the observation tower, peering down at the two boats as they crossed from the airport runway and entered. He acknowledged Zapata's greeting and waved them forward. She had radioed ahead to say that she would be bringing three civilians, a dog and a dead body into the secure compound.

In an open area that normally sheltered the big personal transporters, four young marines waited for Zapata's arrival. None looked especially pleased with their assignment.

Zapata indicated the body lying inside the boat. "Lift it out, and set it on the loading dock," she ordered. "The doctor will be along shortly to take charge of the remains."

The transfer to the loading dock was quicker, and less messy than pulling the corpse out of the water, but the stench soon had the younger guys running for the edge of the platform to puke. She tilted her chin down, hiding a tiny smile. At times like this, she appreciated her cast-iron stomach. Growing up on her father's cattle hacienda had taught her to ignore the disgusting smells and visuals of a messy death. Coupled with her intelligence and quick wit, her calm nature had helped her rise in the male-dominated Navy. Unlike her macho counterparts, she would never tease the younger crewmen about their weak stomachs.

"Okay, good job. Thank you," Zapata said, then turned to Jessica and the guys. "And thank you for your assistance. You were a big help." She reached out a hand and playfully ruffled Sparky's fur. "And you my little friend, are once again a clever detective dog."

Pedro briefly glanced at his hand, checking for gross bits, then offered it to the Lieutenant. "I never did introduce myself properly," he said. "My name is Pedro Velazquez."

"Mucho gusto." She gripped Pedro's hand in a strong handshake, "A pleasure to meet you," she politely replied.

Jessica quickly interjected, "Maricruz, did Pedro tell you he saw a couple of suspicious incidents involving the taxi driver and two men?"

Zapata released Pedro's hand and quirked an eyebrow at him. He looked uncomfortable at being put on the spot. "What did you see?" she asked.

"I'm not sure, perhaps nothing but maybe something," he said. "Somewhere around the middle of the month I saw two men leap out of a battered grey Ford F150 and accost a taxi driver. I don't know if it was the same man, because I didn't notice his cab number."

"Anything else?"

"Just before the storm arrived I was in line for gas at the PeMex station on Aeropuerto Road. The same truck was right in front of my vehicle. The driver did a U-turn and left the line-up."

She shrugged, "Maybe he decided not to wait."

"The same two men were in the truck." Remembering the incident, he scrunched his face in disagreement. "Maybe they didn't like seeing the group of police cruisers and motorcycles in the line ahead of them," Pedro said.

"Yes, that's definitely a possibility. I'll pass the information along to my captain."

"Claro. I also gave the information to Sargent Ramirez of the municipal police."

"Good. Well, I have to get back to work," Zapata said. After spending a little time with the group, she had decided Pedro was probably a decent guy after all. At first he had riled her with his chauvinistic greeting and head-to-toe searching gaze, and she had deliberately not laughed at his lame joke. It had been funny in a weird way. It was the type of humour that first responders indulged in when coping with the messiness of death. She had intended to knock him down a bit, and it seemed to work. He was now treating her with the respect her uniform and rank deserved.

"Perhaps I will run into you at the Loco Lobo sometime," she said.

"I would like that, very much," Pedro said. He was entranced by her warm smile that crinkled the corners of her deep brown eyes. He didn't notice when Jessica grinned and gave Maricruz the thumbs up.

Chapter 30

August 28th – late evening

The house was warm, noisy, jammed with people and over-flowing with mouth-watering smells. Just the way Diego like it. The battery powered lanterns cast a warm glow over everyone, giving the gathering a festive air. If it had been December he would be belting out Christmas carols in his reasonably acceptable tenor voice. Already his residual fear from the previous night's tormenta was dissipating. Life would go on.

He and Yasmin had returned at sundown. He had spent time fiddling with the bilge pump and it was working now. *La Bruja* was in pretty good shape despite the pounding she took. Luis had arrived at the house with the Jeep still in one piece and not too dirty, at least on the inside. He apologized for taking so long to return the vehicle. He had stopped briefly at his cousin Pepe's house to make sure everyone was okay.

Cristina's mom and dad had joined the noisy tumult, playing with their four housebound grandkids. His biggest concern was that no one had heard from Carlos, Pedro or Jessica since the early afternoon. What the hell were they doing?

"Mi amor, sit. Please eat," Cristina said, indicating the plate of food waiting for him.

"Si, thank you, carina," he pulled a chair out and stuffed his muscular thighs under the table.

"They're fine. Don't worry," she murmured in his ear.

He smiled at her. She always was able to read his moods and his thoughts.

"Does anyone know what's going on in Centro?" asked Cristina's dad.

"The Navy officer that we spoke to said there is very bad flooding," Yasmin offered, "but that's all I know."

"And the power is still off all over the island," Diego added, "but other than that we really don't have a good idea of what's happening."

"Maybe we can help with that," said a tired voice.

"Pedro! Carlos! Jessica! Where have you been?" Cristina wrapped her arms about her brother, kissing his cheek, then swapped places with Yasmin to hug and kiss Carlos. Jessica joined the confusion of embraces while Luis and Diego contributed fist-bumps and guy-hugs to the greetings. Pedro bent to smooch his mom's cheek then hugged his dad. Sparky wriggled his way through the throng, gathering pats and head scratches as he greeted everyone in the crowded house.

When the exuberant hubbub died down, Pedro pointed at the plate of food on the table. "Any more of that, sis?" he asked, "we're starving."

"Si, si. José, find more chairs," Cristina said to her son.

Diego reached around Cristina to open the refrigerator. He pulled out three warmish beers, twisted off the tops, and wordlessly passed them over to the new arrivals. "So what's going on?" He pointed at Luis then at the beer, silently asking if he wanted another one. Luis shook his head.

"Serious flooding as Yasmin said, dozens of smashed windows in the taller buildings, no electricity, or other services."

Carlos said, "The roads close to Centro are impassable until you get further south into the higher areas of the colonias."

"Sparky found a corpse floating near the car ferry. It could be the missing taxi driver," Pedro added. "We helped them retrieve the body."

"And Pedro fell in serious lust with the Navy officer," Carlos ping-ponged back into the conversation.

Diego's sputtered beer through his nose, "He what?"

"A beautiful female officer," Jessica added. "My friend, Teniente Maricruz Zapata." Jessica said. "She's gorgeous, but she's no pushover. You had better bring your A-game, bucko," she said to Pedro.

"Si, I got the message, loud and clear," Pedro smiled tiredly at Jessica, then picked up a fork and attacked his plate of spicy ground beef, beans, rice, and tortillas. "This is delicious Cristina. Thank you," he mumbled through a mouthful of food.

Cristina smiled and affectionately patted her brother's broad shoulder.

Jessica discretely lowered a small plate with a mixture of rice and beef to the floor. Sparky sniffed the food.

"How did you get here?" Diego asked, watching as Jessica's dog tentatively sampled the offering. It was a good thing Cristina couldn't see Sparky's hesitant reaction to her delicious cooking. She would be offended that he hadn't instantly gobbled it up and begged for more.

"We used Pa's boat to get to the marina, then rafted it alongside our boat, and walked from there."

"We'll have to scrub the *panga* out tomorrow, it reeks from transporting the corpse," Pedro interjected.

Cristina's face scrunched, "Hermanito, please," she said. "We're eating."

"Sorry sis. I'm tired and didn't think." He looked at his brother-in-law, "By the way, how is *La Bruja*? It was dark and we couldn't tell if she sustained much damage."

"She's survived okay, but she's covered in plant debris and windblown garbage," Diego answered. "Tomorrow we need to open her up to dry out the interior. The bilge pump stopped working at some point during the storm. She has a few nasty scratches on the hull from bashing against the wharf, but otherwise seems okay."

"Well that was lucky."

"God was watching over you," Señora Velazquez said, as she made the sign of the cross.

"Si, of course, Mama," Pedro agreed pleasantly, keeping his eyes discretely aimed at his rapidly disappearing food.

~

Valdez picked his teeth with a dirty fingernail, examined the particle of food and decided it was acceptable. He stuck his finger back in his mouth and sucked the morsel from his nail.

Tormenta Isla

An hour ago he had hammered on his neighbours' door, then banged it wide open before the resident even had a chance to put her hand on the door knob. The woman who lived there was thirty-something, thin, lank-haired and worn-out. Her husband had dumped her and their four scrawny brats six months ago. She was so ugly she wouldn't even qualify as a two-o'clock-beauty-queen, the women who hung around the rough cantinas until last call.

Valdez occasionally paid the woman for sex and a meal, in that order. Today he just wanted the food. He told her he'd come back another time for the screw that she owed him. He belched and patted his gut. Not great food, but filling. Just like humping her, not great but it scratched his itch.

Her little bastards had spent the entire time huddled at one end of the narrow table eyeing his plate. They watched his fork move back and forth like hungry street dogs waiting for scraps. He should have kicked their asses outside, but he couldn't be bothered to expend the energy so he ignored them. Besides, they would whimper and whine and that would drive his blood pressure through the roof necessitating a full on beating to shut them up. It just wasn't worth the effort. Tomorrow there had better be something more than beans and rice for his meal, or he'd spend a little time tuning-up her attitude.

Tormenta Isla

What should he do now? He had zero interest in helping the residents rebuild their pathetic little lives. No one would have the money to hire him. They would want him to help out of the goodness of his heart. Hah. It might be time to relocate.

He still had no way of contacting Don Rafael for more work, or perhaps a temporary loan. Although a loan from his sometimes-employer would come at a huge cost, the interest would be staggering. No, better to just ask for work, not money. He thoughtfully looked at the heavy gold ring on his hand. If all else failed he could pawn it in Cancun, but that would be a last resort. It was a memento from his first kill, one that had nearly cost him his own life, but in the end he was the victor and the other guy was the lump of dead meat.

In the meantime he would hunt around for anything of value to steal. Food, alcohol, money, electronics, drugs. Whatever he could find. He was resourceful. He'd survive.

Chapter 31

August 29th – early morning

Pedro stretched. It had been a good night, no wind, no rain. Back in his own bed he'd slept well. He was a stiff and sore from hefting the two big Yamaha motors out of the bodega and onto the stern of the *panga*. Carlos was doubtlessly suffering as well, being slightly more sedentary with his restaurant business than Diego and he were with their fishing and photography charters.

Today would likely be another day of trying to sort out his life, and to help get the island back to normal as quickly as possible. People needed money to buy groceries. Without the daily influx of tourists things were going to get tense, rapidly. Typically the island had about two million visitors per year. Some were winter residents, others were monthly renters. Then there were the two-week vacationers and the hordes of day-trippers from the Cancun hotel zone. Everyone contributed a little to the island's economy. His biggest concern was how badly Hurricane Pablo had hit Cancun and the airport. Without the infrastructure of a big city and an international airport tourism wouldn't recover quickly.

He really needed information, then smiled when he thought about Teniente Maricruz Zapata. Perhaps she had up-to-date information from the naval outpost on the Cancun side of the bay, it was a satellite of the bigger base on the island. Asking for information would be a plausible reason to contact her. But where did she live? In the Navy housing complex on Rueda Medina near from the marina where *La Bruja* was moored? Or in Centro at the compound where some of the unmarried personal lived?

"Stupid!" he said, slapping himself in the forehead, "I should have asked Jessica last night."

Well, he had his truck, and he could drive over to Jessica's and ask her, or he could get Diego first and work on the boat for a bit. He didn't want to appear to be too eager. He really did want to chat up the intriguing woman and to also find out what was happening in Cancun. He grabbed his keys off the kitchen counter. Jessica's first, then Diego's. On second thought, he would swing by Diego's and tell him what he was up to and arrange a time to work on the boat together.

~

"Woof!"

"Luis is that you?" Jessica asked. Sparky was sniffing along the bottom edge of her front door.

"No, it's me, Jess," Pedro replied.

"Come in," she said opening the door and stepping back. Sparky swirled his tail in his helicopter-mode greeting.

Pedro gave her a light hug and a buss on the cheek, "Your place looks like it survived pretty well," he said, "except the rain has damaged the exterior paint. It's bubbled up and peeled off in a number of places."

"Yep, we did okay. Lots of rain came in under my door. My windows leaked. We had a minor electrical problem when the lightning struck a nearby pole. The backyard is a swamp, but it is slowly draining." She shrugged, "Not bad considering the pounding we took."

"How are you feeling today? You put of a lot of effort into bailing out the half-submerged boat by yourself."

"A little stiff, but that will work itself out." She stretched her arms overhead to relieve some of the soreness.

"A little stiff?" he said with an embarrassed grin, "are you making fun of my dumb-ass joke that no one laughed at?"

Jessica laughed, "No, no. Honestly. I wasn't even thinking of that. Although you did make an ass of yourself with Maricruz," she said.

"I know, I know." he said, then asked, "Where's Luis?"

"He is, but he's out visiting people in the neighbourhood, making sure everyone is okay. Centro is too flooded for him to check his office, but he thinks it will be okay anyway," She said, then pointed at the pile of garbage bags stacked on her sidewalk. "Sparky and I have been cleaning up outside."

Pedro nodded, "My folks are doing the same in our area, checking on the families with young kids and older relatives. Helping out where they can."

"I've had people knocking on my door asking to borrow a shovel, or a rake, or a screwdriver, or a hammer," Jessica said. "They know I like to do my own chores, and have a stash of hand tools," she said with a laugh. "Hopefully most of my tools will come back, but as long as they are being used to help out it really doesn't matter if I get them back or not. I can always buy more."

"Jessica the Tom-boy!" Pedro said.

"The Navy personal came by an hour ago in one of their big grey trucks. They and the Red Cross volunteers are distributing basic foodstuffs like noodles, rice, and sugar to whoever needs it," she said, turning towards her small kitchen area. "I thanked them, but said we are okay for now."

"Si, me too. I passed them on my way here."

"They also told me there is a clinic set up at their main office for free shots for tetanus, flu and hepatitis," she said, "And there is a team of biologists on their way from Mexico City to test the water supply."

"That was quick. I'm impressed," said Diego.

"What are you up to today?" Jessica pointed at a chair, signalling he should sit down and relax for a few minutes. He chose her roomy armchair. It was the only chair in her house that her larger male friends were comfortable using.

"Trying to find out what's happening and then head over to work on the boat with Diego," Pedro said as he sat down. "I'm curious to know if the cadaver Sparky located was the missing taxi driver."

"I bet you are dying of curiosity," she quipped.

"And you think my jokes are bad," Pedro groaned. "I was thinking the folks at the Navy base would have a better idea by now how bad the damage is in Cancun."

She grinned, "We could ask Teniente Zapata for information."

He flushed a deeper colour, "Am I that obvious?"

"Only a little, but it's a good idea."

"Do you know where she might be?"

"She lives in the big orange compound, near the collection of marinas along Laguna Makax." Jessica checked the time by glancing at her kitchen clock. It was an archaic device in a world of smartphones but the inexpensive, spur-of-the-moment purchase had turned to be a good decision. "As you know, she worked late last night, so maybe she's still sleeping."

"I doubt any of the Navy personal, or other emergency workers are sleeping in today," he said, "it'll be all hands on deck, pardon the lame pun."

"Ah, but I have her phone number," said Jessica, playfully wig-wagging her phone in the air.

Pedro grinned at her, "How are you going to call her?"

Jessica looked at her device, then shook her head. "I keep forgetting we don't have cell phone service." She propped her chin on her fist, "I suppose you could drive me to the compound entrance and I could ask the gate guard if Maricruz was home."

Pedro considered the idea, then shook his head, "No, I don't want to look like a desperate stalker by going to her residence." Pedro leaned forward and rested his forearms on his knees.

"Okay, then if you don't have any immediate plans why don't we round up Luis and do a little cleanup around the neighbourhood?"

He shook his head again, "I can't. I promised Diego I would help him with our boat today. You and Luis can borrow my truck, but first please drop me off at the marina."

~

At the Marina Makax Diego climbed onto *La Bruja*, his weight causing the big boat to dip slightly. Noticing Pedro's worried scrutiny of the deep scratches in the hull he said, "It looks a lot worse than it is."

"Do you want to start cleaning her up here, or move her to our regular spot first?" Pedro stood with his fists resting on his hip bones, surveying the muck and mess strewn across the decks of his baby. Other guys had love affairs with their cars, his first love was this boat. Even though he was partners with Diego, he loved *La Bruja* as if she was all his. His mistress.

"The wharf here is usable, and we don't know the situation with our normal berth. We had better leave her here until we know for sure that it's safe to move her."

"Claro," Pedro stuck his head inside the salon, and blew out a sigh of frustration, "all that cleaning we did a few days ago was just wasted energy."

Diego laughed, "You sound like Cristina when she grouses about washing the dishes - every day, all year around." He waved a hand towards the interior of the boat, "Come on *princesa*. We have work to do."

"*Pendejo*," Pedro said with a chuckle in his voice. "Let's open her up and get the air flowing through."

"You put the cushions on the foredeck to dry in the sun. I'll re-check the bilge to be sure she isn't leaking then remove the window protectors."

Chapter 32

August 30th – morning

Ramirez laced up his high, black leather boots then stamped each foot twice to settle the footwear more comfortably. Then he stuffed his work related items into his pockets. Police ID and wallet went into the front right-hand side. Keys for the house and personal vehicle on the left. Handcuffs, work keys and the police issue flashlight hung on his thick leather utility belt. At the station he would sign out a radio and a pistol to add to the weight, causing him to walk with a gun-slinger's swagger. He turned to Alexis, "Ready?"

"Almost done, just a couple of more minutes," she said.

Ramirez smiled as Alexis pulled her flowing dark hair into a messy ponytail, securing it with one of those cloth-covered scrunchey things she liked to use. The females in Mexican police force didn't have to wear their hair in short unfeminine styles, even though occasionally during an arrest an offender had been known to grab a female constable by the hair. Typically when that happened, the culprit would, in the end, be more injured than the constable. The women looked soft, but they were as tough as the men.

"At least we now know happened to Ricardo Villarreal," he said, leaning against the bathroom sink while he waited for Alexis. "That's one part of the mystery solved. Now, we have to find out who killed him."

"It was lucky the corpse got caught against the fencing, and didn't float away otherwise we would never know what happened to him." She gently shoved her mate aside, "move over, I need a mirror for a minute."

"You're perfect, you don't have to check," he said as he shifted his bulk sideways. She flicked him an appreciative smile.

Apparently satisfied with what she saw she turned away from the mirror and began to load her utility belt and pockets with her equipment, "Whose dog alerted the searchers?"

"The blonde woman who works at the Loco Lobo. I think her name is Jessica Sanderson. The dog's name is Sparky, *Chispito*," Ramirez answered, then added, "the captain informed Villarreal's wife last night."

"I've never done a NOK, she said referring to a next of kin notification. It would be difficult telling a family member their loved one is dead."

"Si, I agree. Are you ready now carina?"

"Alright, let's get back at it," she said.

The last few days had been an endless procession of work, eat, sleep, work, eat, sleep and the added stress of worrying about their parents and younger siblings. Neither he nor Alexis had children from their previous relationships, although he sure wouldn't mind having a couple of kids underfoot. He loved getting sloppy kisses from small smelly bodies and listening to their sweet little voices recount in minute detail their extremely fascinating day. His desire to have a family was a conversation for another day.

He wrapped his arms around her compact form and gave her a long, loving smooch. "It'll get better soon," he said.

"You are always so irritatingly optimistic, Filipe," she said, poking him in the ribs with her elbow. Her eyes flashed with humour.

"That's me, Señor Optimista," he answered, dodging another poke from her elbow.

~

Carlos pulled open the side entrance to the Loco Lobo. The sea level had finally receded giving him the opportunity to get inside the restaurant and begin the process of re-opening his business. The street and the floors inside were covered in a slippery mix of sand, small pieces of coral, seaweed, plastic bottles and other garbage that had blown or floated through Centro.

Yasmin trundled behind him, wearing a set of plastic boots that she had found at the Chedraui grocery store. Designed for kids the gumboots were decorated with yellow ducks and she felt ridiculous wearing them. With only her moto for transportation, Carlos had good-naturedly perched on the passenger's seat and refrained from commenting on her odd footwear, and her clumsy gear changes.

"So far I'm not seeing too much damage," she said scrutinizing the inside of the building.

"No, it's not bad," he agreed. "The benefit of concrete floors and concrete walls."

"Filthy dirty, a few dead fish, and a high water mark along the walls." She said, pointing to the dirty line about chest-height. "What about the photos?" she said indicating the collection of images secured to the walls.

"They are printed on, lona, outdoor canvas. A cleaning with soap and water and they should be fine. But I'm worried about the motors for the fridges, dishwasher and walk-in cooler," Carlos said, walking towards the kitchen area.

"Without electricity how can you test them?"

"Can't really, but we need to get everything cleaned up so that Santiago can service the motors before the electricity is restored." Carlos said.

"Carlos are you here?" Asked a voice.

"Hola, Juan," he responded to his head chef. "Come in, the side gate is open."

The short round-faced man trudged inside, peering unhappily at the kitchen. "Big mess," he said succinctly.

"Si, big mess," Carlos agreed, "But more importantly how are you and your family?"

Juan shrugged, "wet and tired, but okay."

"That's very good to hear," Carlos said, adding, "We could sure use a few more hands to help clean up."

Yasmin studied the chef's face, he looked as if he hadn't slept for a week. She remembered he had a young wife and two toddlers at home and they had probably been terrified during the storm. She knew she had been petrified when the broken power pole had landed with an earth-shaking thump on Carlos' car.

"And we could really use more buckets, mops, rags," she added, hoping she wasn't being too pushy.

Juan nodded, indicating he had heard her, "I'll do what I can, but finding supplies and more people will take time. Everyone will be busy sorting out their own homes."

"I understand." Carlos replied. "Just see what you can do, but don't waste all your gas running around the island. We'll start with what we have."

"Okay, see you later." Juan said, turning around and heading towards the street.

"I think a hose would be quicker." Yasmin quipped as she opened a storage cupboard and pulled out a bucket and mop.

Carlos stopped and looked at her, "Brilliant idea. Fresh water isn't going to do anymore damage."

"Except of course ... we don't have any water pressure," she said indicating the trickle of water coming from the bar sink tap, "just the pressure from the water in the *tinaco*," meaning the large plastic storage tank on the roof of the restaurant.

"Ah ..." he stopped mid-curse shoving both hands through his thick hair and snorted out a frustrated explosion, "... damn it!"

Chapter 33

August 31st

Eyeing the outside of his office building for damage Luis didn't see the long, shard of glass on the sidewalk.

"Luis, watch out," Jessica shouted, reaching for him as his foot awkwardly slid out from under him.

He cursed softly as his knees made contact with the glass and the muddy sidewalk. Using the wall he steadied himself and regained his feet. He quickly glanced at hands, they were scuffed but not cut. His leg hurt like hell and it was bleeding. If he had been wearing his slacks instead of shorts the fabric might have saved his skin.

"Let me see," Jessica said, putting her hand on his arm to hold him still. "You have a long gash across the front of your leg. You're bleeding."

"Don't worry, I'm fine. My blood clots quickly," he said, dismissively. "I just want to see how bad the damage is inside.

He limped to the door, and fiddled with the thumbscrews. The long thin metal rod that secured the top half to the top of the door frame, dropped down with a clang. He slid the bottom rod up a few inches and retightened the thumbscrew, holding the rod in place and free of the concrete door sill. Pushing back the cortina, he unlocked his front door and paused.

"Stand to the side while I open the door. There could be a lot of water trapped inside," He said, motioning her to move to the right.

"Sure," Jessica said as she picked her way through the broken glass to stand out of the way. "I'm really glad we left Sparky at home. He would have cut his paws to ribbons walking on this stuff."

Luis nodded, "It will be a few days before the city folks can get this all cleared up. Although the islanders will pitch in, helping out where they can. They always do." He cautiously cracked the door open. Only a thin trickle of muddy water oozed over the sill.

"Not too bad inside." He said, pushing the door wide open. The floor had a slimy film of fine silt that had been forced through the spaces around the entrance and windows by the flooding. Fortunately the *cortinas* had managed to keep the windows intact and the damage inside was minimal.

"Your windows are okay. I wonder where the glass is from."

"The wind can carry it quite a distance," Luis said. He looked up, then pointed at a small condo complex a few lots south that hadn't been completely boarded over. It was missing a handful of windows. "It could have come from that building."

Jessica carefully walked across the slippery tile floor, heading towards the staff washroom in search of clean paper towels. A thin line of blood was still dribbling down the front of Luis' leg. She pulled off several pieces of paper and retraced her steps. "Sit down for a couple of minutes, please."

"Jess, really, I'm okay."

"Sit! Let me have a look," she pointed at a relatively clean chair.

With a smile tugging at the corner of his mouth he felt the chair cushion, decided it was only damp not soaking wet and obediently sat down.

Dabbing at the cut she could see it wasn't deep enough to require stitches but it did need to be bandaged. "Where do you keep your first aid kit?" she asked glancing up at him. "I need some antiseptic, two or three sterile pads, and a roll of gauze to hold them in place."

"I don't have one."

"What do you do when you cut yourself?"

"Let it bleed. Or rip off a clean piece of an old t-shirt and tie that over the cut."

"Luis, really?" Jessica huffed. "This cut needs to be cleaned and covered. There are at least ten billion germs in that muck," she said pointing to the brown puddle where his knee had contacted the glass. "It's a toxic stew of sewerage overflow and dead things."

His dark brown eyes twinkled with laughter, "I understand, Doctor Sanderson, but I wasn't expecting to require expert medical attention. I don't have a first aid kit."

She snorted a laugh and lightly slapped his arm, "Jerk."

~

Rafael Fernandez leaned back in his comfortable chair and put his feet up on an empty wooden crate. He watched the man in front of him as a snake would study a mouse. As he cleaned his fingernails with his favourite folding knife, more for effect than necessity, he enjoyed watching Fernando Sánchez's frantic eyes follow every move of his hands.

They were inside one of his large empty warehouses located on the outskirts of Cancun, far away from neighbours who might overhear disturbing noises, not that he cared either way. His paid police informers would quickly tell him who complained and where they lived. He enjoyed his hard-earned reputation for being a truly evil man, and any sensible person would never risk annoying him. If they weren't smart enough to keep their heads down and avoid coming to his attention, he would suggest to his employees that the busybodies should be culled. It was a reminder to the rest of the herd to forget the sights and sounds that were none of their business in the first place.

Clean a nail, inspect it. Clean another nail, inspect that one. With eight more nails to attend to his guest might die of a stroke before he had finished his manicure. The man stank of fear and piss.

"Are you comfortable my friend?" Fernandez asked.

A muffled grunt was the response. Sánchez was tightly bound to a metal chair, a rancid cloth stuffed in his mouth prevented him from speaking.

"I have heard from my friends in the policiá that the little problem you and Valdez were supposed to take care of has re-surfaced."

Sánchez desperately worked his tongue, trying to push the gag out of his mouth. Fernandez knew the man wanted to plead his case, to promise anything in return for being allowed to live. Disappointingly he had seldom met a man brave enough to hold his gaze when the man realized his life was about to end badly.

Fernandez tilted his chin at the man standing behind the chair. A large brown hand reached around and shoved the gag further down Sánchez's throat cutting off his air supply. Sánchez tossed his head from side to side, frantically trying to dislodge the obstruction.

Don Rafael waited a minute or two then said to his subordinate, "Not yet, Alfonso. Fernando and I haven't finished our little chat."

Alfonso pulled the gag back a bit. Sánchez greedily gulped in air.

"Now as I was saying, my problem has re-surfaced," Fernandez pointed the sharp knife at his prisoner. "So, first of all I want my money returned, plus interest. Secondly, I want you to kill Valdez."

Sánchez nodded eagerly. His eyes were filled with apprehensive hope.

Rafael's flat stare flicked briefly up to meet the gaze of the man standing behind Sánchez. A cunning look passed between them. They both knew Don Rafael was merely toying with their captive. Sánchez wasn't going to leave this room, or even that chair, alive. He would be unrecognizable by the time Fernandez had finished amusing himself.

Chapter 34

September 2nd - morning

"Come on boys, time for a short pee walk. I have to go back to work soon. There's more cleaning to do at the Loco Lobo," Jessica said to Sparky and Max. Sparky helpfully stepped into his harness, left front paw first, then his right paw.

Her second rescue dog, Max, was still recovering from his injuries. He waited patiently while she gently lifted his feet and inserted them through the nylon loops.

"You're getting fat, Maxie," she said, tugging on the harness until she could snap together the two ends of the buckle.

Several people in Max's old neighbourhood had recognized him from her 'found dog' posters plastered on walls and utility poles. The consensus was he didn't have an owner and for the last five years he had somehow scrounged enough food to survive as a street dog.

People in the area had called him Max, so that was what she was calling him, although a better name for him would have been

Hoover. The dog loved to eat, and could vacuum up anything that even remotely resembled food; smelly things pulled out of garbage cans, small and very dead lizards, and occasionally cat turds. Maybe that's why one of the part-time gringo residents had affectionately nicknamed him the Fuzzy Turd. With a collection of their own dogs back home she and her husband were unable to adopt Max, but had supplied him with food, water, and affection whenever possible.

Whatever his name he was frightened of people, especially men. He was slowly adjusting to living indoors, learning not to do his business inside the house. He recently had let Luis pat his head and scratch his ears. They were making steady progress.

For Jessica, life was good. The sun was shining, she had food to eat, a place to live, and friends who loved her. She had even found a way to get a message to her family via the Canadian Consulate in Cancun that she was safe and doing well. She still had a job, although it was not exactly lucrative at the moment. No customers meant no tips, but Carlos was trying his best to keep everyone employed.

Carlos had decided that the Loco Lobo would soon be able to offer simple meals during daylight hours using whatever ingredients were available. The big grocery store, Chedraui, had generators running with enough power to offer a limited amount of fresh meat and vegetables. He planned to shop daily and stop serving food when everything had been consumed. Ice was still not available anywhere on the island.

A few feet from the house Sparky stopped abruptly, planting his solid little body in his wait-a-minute stance. Jessica tugged lightly on his leash, "come on Sparky."

Jessica tugged again but he still ignored her, staring at a car that was turning around in the street. The front end of the vehicle bounced against a discarded matrimonial-sized mattress, what she would have called a double. For the last few days it had been propped against an outside wall and left for the municipal garbage collectors to wrestle with on the next large-item pick up day. The weight of the water had sagged the discarded bed, bending it in the middle then it had plopped over into the road, much too heavy for one person to lift.

As the driver completed his turn the mattress slid between the two front-wheels and then snagged on something underneath. The driver impatiently accelerated, shoving the heavy obstruction along the road a ways.

Jessica dropped the leashes to the ground and placed her foot firmly on the ends. She frantically waved both arms over her head.

"Stop! Stop!"

The car stopped, and both men peered quizzically through the windshield at her. She could almost read the words on their lips. "What does the *gringa loca,* want?"

She pointed, indicating the road in front of the car then gathered up the dog leashes.

The doors opened simultaneously and two sets of high-top black boots thumped on to the ground. Dressed in the black State Police uniforms with large revolvers strapped to their legs, the unsmiling men had a slightly menacing air about them. The passenger was a middle-aged, rotund man. The driver, tall and lean, had a precisely trimmed pencil-thin moustache decorating his upper lip. They glared at her.

Jessica didn't recognize either man from the State Police contingent based on the island so perhaps they were some of the officers sent from other cities to help out. She motioned to the front of the car again. They strode around the open doors to the front of their vehicle and looked to where she was pointing. Max pulled sharply on his leash trying to get away from the formidable figures coming his way.

"Todo bien, todo bien," she said quietly, trying to calm the wild-eyed, whimpering pooch.

The driver muttered something to his partner and he returned to the vehicle, while the other man gripped the wet, and now filthy mattress with both hands.

The older man braced his feet and nodded. "Okay."

The moustachioed man gunned the engine in reverse, dragging his startled partner and the sodden bed backwards a car length before abruptly stopping. In danger of smashing face-first into the grill of the cruiser, the older man slammed his hands down on the hood of the car and glared at the younger driver.

"Wait. *Momentito,*" Jessica said, fighting a giggle, desperately trying not to laugh at the unsmiling men. Keeping the two dog leashes wound around her left hand she knelt in front of the car and reached her right arm deep under the vehicle, then she pushed down on the material hooked on the front sway bar. Feeling the fabric rip free, she swept her hand underneath to ensure there were no other problems and then pulled herself upright. She and the dogs stepped onto the sidewalk, and she nodded at the hefty, older man, "It's okay now."

"Gracias," he mumbled without making eye contact, and slammed the car door.

The driver accelerated rapidly backwards, then turned sharply to the left and swerved around the obstruction. They sped away from the embarrassing situation, as

Tormenta Isla

Jessica bent over double with laughter. Sparky excitedly danced around his tail swirling in helicopter mode. Max stared after the departing car. He seemed to be wondering what all the fuss was about.

Jessica was wiping the tears from her eyes when her neighbours poked their heads outside to investigate.

Try as she might, Jessica couldn't stop the laughter bubbling over again as she described the scenario to her friends. They were still giggling when they separated, going into their own homes.

Chapter 35

September 5th

Valdez felt his stomach cramp with hunger. He hadn't eaten for two days. No matter how often he thumped the woman who usually scraped together meals for him, she still couldn't find anything to cook. Even the few scrawny chickens that normally roamed the colonia had mysteriously disappeared. Looking out through the empty space that had been his doorway he avoided her pleading gaze. He couldn't stand the sound of her four brats crying and snivelling about being hungry. It wasn't his problem if she and the little bastards were starving. Her kids. Her problem.

His grabbed his keys, patted the pocket where he kept his knife and walked outside to his truck. Turning the key in the ignition he glanced at the gas gauge. He still had about a quarter of a tank. No one in the neighbourhood dared to siphon his fuel but he certainly didn't mind helping himself to someone else's supply. He opened the glove box, ensuring the piece of plastic tubing was still there. The sun would be setting in fifteen minutes giving him the opportunity to refill his gas tank, then head out to find food.

Tormenta Isla

He had seen the passenger boats bringing supplies to the island. The big grocery store had a generator supplying enough electricity to keep a few lights and a couple of refrigerators working but most of the smaller stores were only selling non-perishable food items. Someone somewhere on the island would have at least the basics of rice, beans, and tortillas. Fortunately most of the islanders prepared food on propane stoves or charcoal grills which didn't require electricity to function. With any luck he might find a bit of cooked meat. Beef, pork, chicken, fish, turtle or iguana. It didn't matter as long as it was protein. Well, not dog, cat or rat – he wasn't that desperate, yet.

Driving towards Punta Sur past the big houses set along the cliff, Valdez wondered if any of the owners had stayed or had scampered back to safety in Gringoland. The large decorative houses on both sides of the road were boarded over, or protected by hurricane *cortinas*. There didn't appear to be much structural damage in this area except for the inevitable broken power poles and downed lines. There were no signs of repairs or cleanup attempts as yet. This area was primarily the playground of foreigners, and would be last on the list to be restored.

The heavily populated Centro and the colonias, where the bulk of the working population lived, would get first priority. But he was hoping that he could find a way into a few of the houses to search for small electronics, food and of course alcohol. It all depended on how rapidly the owners or renters vacated the premises when the advisory went out to evacuate the island.

Valdez slowed his truck and turned into a long pathway that ran across the federal zone in front of two or three dozen expensive homes built by foreigners. Stopping in front of an empty lot with a tangle of palm trees and thick prickly bushes he slowly nosed the truck deep into the undergrowth. The sharp thorns screeched as they dug into the patches of sun-bleached paint that clung tenaciously to his vehicle. It was a good spot to stash the pickup while he searched for a way inside one of the houses.

He paused and listened. The night was blissfully quiet and dark. No bright lights, or loud music, or drunken voices. Only the rattling buzz of the recently hatched cicadas as they swarmed the branches of wind-damaged trees. After they devoured the tattered green remnants they would search for a mate then die shortly afterwards. The birds, lizards and stray cats would eat well for a few days, dining on cicadas. He briefly thought about capturing a few, pulling the wings off and eating their protein-filled bodies, but the mere idea made him gag.

He stepped over a gate flattened by the storm. A crushed limestone pathway contrasted with the darker vegetation, guiding his way around the side of the house. He pushed and pulled handles, then yanked on the edges of the metal *cortinas* covering windows and patio doors. Nothing came loose.

He searched along an overgrown pathway on the north side of the house, discovering a hidden side entrance that hadn't been boarded up. It had been overlooked in the rush to secure the house before the storm hit the island. He picked up a large rock, Valdez set to work smashing an insubstantial doorknob. It always amused him when people spent a fortune on complicated locks for the main entrance, but used cheaper options for less visible doorways. This one was conveniently hidden by an overgrown garden. A few hard hits and the handle fell off. He stuck a finger inside the hole and manipulated the lock mechanism, opening the door.

"*¡Pasa, por favor!* Please come in," he murmured, then replied, "I will. Thank you very much."

The entrance led him into a laundry area, then a bedroom, and finally into the living area. A quick search revealed an over-sized television, too big to carry by himself. He ignored it. He was looking for smaller items that could be converted to cash or food. He headed into the kitchen, pulling open the refrigerator door. The smell of rotting meat greeted his nostrils. He fanned the stench away from his face and searched for anything edible. A soft apple, a greasy hunk of orange cheese that didn't smell too bad, a handful of puckered grapes and an opened package of sliced ham. He sniffed the odorous meat, reluctantly tossing it back inside the refrigerator. He was hungry but wasn't about to risk being poisoned by spoiled meat.

There was one can of Corona Lite. He popped the top and tipped the can back. Warm beer flooded his mouth as he gulped the contents. It tasted like piss, but he could feel the alcohol fizzing in his blood. He burped, then wiped the back of his hand across his mouth. About a dozen more of those, and he'd feel half-way human again.

He flung his bits of food onto the nearby table, then pulled out his knife intending to cut the cheese and apple into chunks. The dark stain on the knife blade reminded him that he hadn't cleaned it since he'd slit Villarreal's throat two weeks ago. He shrugged, and sliced into the apple.

While he chewed his meagre meal he thought about Fernando Sánchez, the guy who helped him kill the taxi driver. "Humph, wonder where that *pendejo* is now?" he muttered to himself. "He's probably hiding from the hurricane on the mainland.

Then his thoughts turned again to Don Rafael. He had to get his ass in gear and find a way to contact the man. The electricity and phones were still out. The passenger boats were sporadically ferrying people between the island and the mainland, but he didn't have any money to purchase a ride. So, getting a hold of cash was his next goal. Cash for the boat ride, taxi fares in Cancun, and maybe a cold beer or two.

Strobing red and blue lights reflected through two narrow glass panels on either side of the front door.

"Policiá!" Valdez said forcefully, like a person who discovered they had stepped in a pile of fresh dog shit.

He folded his knife, stuffed it in his right-hand pocket and swiftly eased through the damaged side door. He dodged through the knotted vegetation towards the pathway on the ocean-side of the house. The policiá were just doing a drive-by along the main road, but he wasn't about to be trapped like a rat in a maze, with only one way in and one way out. He crouched beside the driver's side of his truck, waiting for the police to pass by. The cops inside the cab would be scanning the roadway ahead, while the ones in the back of the pickup searched both sides of the road for suspicious activities.

He didn't want to make any move that would attract the eye of the cops riding in the back. The strobing lights carried on past the municipal landfill, and disappeared from his line of sight. He let out his breath with a quiet sigh. His hunger was momentarily dulled by the overripe cheese and fruit. He'd have to keep trying houses until he could get his hands on cash.

Chapter 36

September 8th

"Yes! Electricity!" Jessica shouted. She and Yasmin were sorting supplies at the Loco Lobo restocking everything in preparation for the expected resumption of the electrical power when one overhead light unexpectedly flickered to life. It had been a long two weeks since Hurricane Pablo had torn down lines and poles, island-wide.

"Thank goodness. Maybe we can have hot showers tonight," Yasmin replied.

Many islanders had decided to go for a daily swim in the ocean and leave what little water they had remaining in their *tinaco* for other uses like brushing their teeth, flushing toilets and washing dishes. Aguakan, the water and waste company, had been able to bring a trailer-mounted generator to the island to keep the waste water system working in the areas of the island that had sewer lines. The water supplied by the underwater pipe from Cancun had been restored five days after the storm, but anyone with a personal pressure system that required electricity was out of luck. An insipid trickle of cool water was all that emerged from kitchen taps and bathroom shower heads.

"Let's see if we can get any of the other lights working." Jessica put down the armload of paper towel rolls. She searched along the shelving until she found a package of twelve fluorescent globes. She picked up the step ladder and set it up under an overhead fixture. "Can you hold the ladder for me?" she asked climbing to the rung, second from the top.

"Are we going to get a shock?" asked Yasmin, eyeing Jessica's hand as it inched towards the metal light fixture.

"You shouldn't, the ladder has a sticker on the side saying it is shock resistant, but, I might," she added as she warily tapped the metal fixture with her knuckles testing to see if she would get a shock. She didn't know if it was just an old wives tale, but she had been told never to touch a suspect surface with her fingers. Something about an electrical short might cause her hand to reflexively curl and grab the surface. If she used the back side of her hand would it hopefully have the reverse effect and knock her hand away. Still, electrical shorts scared the bejesus out of her.

"I think it's okay," Jessica said, then unscrewed the bulb and reinserted a fresh one. The lamp illuminated. "Yes!"

"When did the power come back on?" Carlos poked his head out of the gloomy kitchen.

"About five minutes ago."

"How did you know it was on?" he asked, walking through the restaurant flicking switches.

"That light came on," she pointed at the ceiling fixture." I might have flipped the wall switch on at some point," Yasmin answered. "It's a habit."

"Claro, good to know we have power," Carlos said. He stared up at the few overhead lights that glowed dully. "I'm not sure if the amperage is strong enough to run the compressors on the fridges. Leave all appliances unplugged for now."

"Sure," Jessica agreed, "I'll try to get a couple of lights in the kitchen area working."

"I can do it," Carlos said holding out his hand for the carton.

"No, I've got this." Jessica said ignoring his outstretched hand. She folded the ladder and moved towards the kitchen area, calling out to Juan, "Hey, chef. Permission to enter your kingdom?"

"Si, come in," Juan said with a chuckle in his voice. He motioned her inside.

Jessica tipped a smile at the man. In the past he had been aloof and downright chauvinistic towards her. But since the storm his attitude had slowly improved as he watched the women pitch in with the hard dirty work of cleaning and organizing the restaurant. "I only have a few spare bulbs. Pick three lights and I will see if we can get them working."

He pointed at the fixtures, then moved aside to allow the women to set up their ladder.

Ten minutes later, Jessica stepped off the ladder, "Et voila!" she said in French, sweeping her hand in a grand flourish.

"*Mande*? What?" Juan asked, his eyebrows pinched together in a question.

"There you go!" she repeated in English.

"Ah, gracias. Muchas gracias."

~

Using her cellphone Constable Alexis Gomez snapped a photo of the smashed door handle. "What's this, break-in number thirty?" she asked Ramirez, as she pushed the door open and entered the house.

"Thirty that we have responded to," he said, "but there have been hundreds more."

"Who called this one in?" she asked, taking more photos of interior. Personal cellphones were their only method of recording a crime scene.

"Their maintenance guy. He came out to check for the owners who are in the US. He discovered the smashed doorknob and did a quick walk-through looking for other damage."

"Why didn't he secure the door somehow?" she stuck her head into the big bathroom attached to the bedroom. Everything looked okay there.

"He's gone to look for a sheet of plywood. He didn't have anyone to leave at the house. All of the adults in his family are either fixing their homes, or babysitting other houses that have been broken into."

"Everyone is looking for the same thing, money and food." A large television was mounted on the living room wall. Alexis pointed at it, "I'm surprised someone hasn't helped themselves to that yet."

"Too big, not worth much at the moment," Ramirez said, then paused beside the mess on the kitchen table. "Someone was hungry, but left in a big hurry. That's a good-sized chunk of cheese that he wasted," he said pointing at the insect-covered mound of orange gunk.

Alexis snapped a few more photos, and scratched a note in her book. "We could call in the CSI team, plus the fingerprint experts, and maybe the burglary team. They could solve the crime in the one hour allotted to this week's episode," she said.

Ramirez snorted. He flicked her an amused glance.

In truth the municipal police had very limited training, and almost nothing in the way of equipment to assist them with solving crimes. It was a ridiculous situation. Even their breathalyzer 'test' was a command for a suspected drunk driver to blow into the cop's hands, then the constable would sniff for excessive alcohol. Their station had been equipped with one breathalyzer for a few short months with only one test straw that was to be re-used time and again. When numerous complaints surfaced on social media about this unsanitary practice they were forced to stop using the device.

"Should we wait for the guy to get back?" she asked pocketing her phone and notebook.

"No, not our problem. Dispatch has a backup of calls for us to attend to," Ramirez said, clumping noisily towards the exit. "The owners will get a file number for their insurance claim. That's all we can do."

"You hear anything new on the Ricardo Villarreal murder case?"

"Nothing yet. I'm still keeping my eye out for the driver of that ratty grey pickup that

Pedro told me about. I really want to talk to that guy."

"Why?"

"He and another guy got into a nasty altercation with Villarreal a day or two before he went missing. Too big a coincidence. And," he tapped his large blade-shaped nose, "my big ugly cop's nose doesn't like coincidences. Not at all."

Chapter 37

September 10th

Maricruz Zapata sucked on the straw, noisily draining the last of her Coke from the glass. She idly glanced around the Loco Lobo, watching as Jessica effortlessly delivered a tray of food and beverages to a nearby table of four middle-aged customers. They looked like they were experienced tourists who were happy to take advantage of the super cheap hotel deals being offered in an attempt to entice visitors back to the tattered island.

Thankfully the Cancun airport had only been closed for a couple of days while the runways were cleared of debris and the electricity restored, and tourists were starting to trickle back into the area. It was amazing how a category five hurricane could cut a path of destruction in one area, and leave another area completely alone. Odd things happened during a hurricane like a beachfront home on the eastern side had sustained only one cracked window, while a brand new house located high up on the western side was completed gutted by the fierce winds.

She fiddled with her phone, swiping the screen to see if she could connect to the restaurant's internet. The signal connected briefly then blinked out again. How did people manage to stay in touch before the internet? Before smartphones? She caught a stealthy movement in the corner of her eye and quickly turned her head to see a lean, scruffy man reaching over the bar, sweeping his hand in a searching motion. He snatched up the small metal box that the staff were temporarily using for cash while the electronic cash register was being repaired.

"Hey!" She yelled, pointing at the man.

The man sliced a quick feral glance at her and ran into the street, clutching the box close to his body with one arm.

"Stop thief!" Maricruz leapt to her feet, her hand reaching for her service revolver as her brain relayed the message - civilian clothes, not armed. "Jessica! Yasmin! Call the cops." She sped after the man, sprinting along Hidalgo Avenue.

"Maricruz, wait!" Jessica yelled, then tossed aside her empty tray and ran after her friend.

Yasmin punched 911 into her phone. Nothing. No signal. "Carlos?" she shouted.

"What's going on?"

"I think some guy grabbed our cash. Maricruz and Jessica are chasing him." She pointed north on Hidalgo. "I can't get through to the police."

"*Madre de Dios*, he's probably got a knife." He reached behind the bar and snatched up the baseball bat that he recently stashed there.

"Oh shit, oh shit," Yasmin muttered as he joined the chase. She tried 911 again. The number rang, then disconnected.

~

Maricruz breathed deeply and evenly as she ran. She normally ran from Playa Norte to Punta Sur and back, about fourteen kilometers, as part of her daily fitness routine. Slowly gaining ground she noticed the man was breathing heavily, as if he didn't have good lung capacity or maybe he was a smoker. Got you now, you bastard. She could see his long ropy arm muscles and wide knotted shoulders, the result of hard physical work not hours spent in a gym. *Take him down from the back. Keep those arms away from my neck.*

Still moving forward the man swiveled his head from side to side as if he was searching for an exit.

Increasing her speed Maricruz sprang into the air and slammed both feet into the centre of his back.

He grunted and fell face first onto the pavement. The cash box clattered to the pavement and burst open spilling a handful of coins and paper money onto the street.

A tourist screamed.

Maricruz landed with both knees driving hard into his spine. He grunted a curse. She grabbed his right arm, rotating it between his shoulder blades and yanked hard.

A shopkeeper ran outside, "How can I help?"

"Maricruz!" yelled Jessica as she raced forward.

"Stomp on his left arm."

"Got it," Jessica shouted as her foot made contact, beating the shopkeeper's foot by what seemed like a millisecond.

"I'll kill you," the man roared as he attempted to twist and flip Maricruz off his back.

"Shut up!" Carlos arrived clenching the baseball bat in his right hand. He whacked the end against the man's ass, "and stay still," he ordered, "or I will use your *cojones* for batting practice."

"Stand on his thighs, Carlos, don't let him get up," Maricruz ordered. "He's strong."

Carlos and the shopkeeper pressed one foot on each of the man's knee joints, eliciting a stream of threats. "Anyone get through to the police?" he asked.

"Not yet, I've been a little busy," Maricruz replied, a light hint of sarcasm in her voice.

"Claro." Keeping his eyes on the man Carlos pulled his phone out of his pocket and swiped at the screen. "It's ringing," he said. "Hopefully the signal will last."

"Bueno," Maricruz replied. Out of the corner of her eye she noticed the breeze was toying with the paper money, playfully threatening to blow the few bits of paper back towards the Loco Lobo. Hardly enough to be worth all this effort.

~

Sergeant Ramirez, placed a booted foot on the bumper of his cruiser while he scribbled a few notes.

His eyes skimmed over the trim, dark-haired woman standing a few feet away. She was dressed in snugly fitting shorts, a skimpy tank-top and a pair of light canvas shoes. When he had arrived on the scene and taken control of her captive, she had identified herself as a lieutenant in the Marinas. Ramirez had cocked an eyebrow and suspiciously demanded to see her identification.

She had slowly spun in a circle, with her arms held away from her torso and asked, "Do you see anywhere on my body where I might be hiding my identification, Sergeant?"

Holding her challenging gaze, Ramirez had swallowed his laughter. In his peripheral vision he could see his partner, Alexis, tense at the playful interaction between him and the lieutenant. He was going to get an earful from Alexis, when they were out of range of the others.

Both Carlos Mendoza and Jessica Sanderson had provided their identification and confirmed the woman really was a teniente, and she had had a good reason to chase and subdue the man.

"Teniente Zapata," Ramirez said, as he tucked his notebook and pen in his shirt pocket, "nice take down."

"Gracias Sergeant." she replied, then tipped back a bottle of cool water, half-draining it before pausing for a breath.

The others had returned to the Loco Lobo, having given their statements. The metal container and the small amount of cash had been bagged as evidence. Carlos had shrugged indifferently.

"We've been looking for Señor Valdez." Ramirez pointed his finger at the man who was handcuffed to the bench in the back of the police pickup. A stone-faced constable sat on either side, glaring at their prisoner.

Maricruz paused with the water bottle near her lips. "Really? Why?"

"Do you remember that body that was found on August 28th, near the car ferry parking lot?"

"Of course," she retorted. "It's a little unusual to find a stiff floating in the roadway." Intrigued at what Ramirez might add, she studied his expression as she slowly lowered the water bottle and replaced the cap. "What does that have to do with this man?"

Ramirez replied, "We have information that indicates this man is the killer."

Maricruz blinked, then tipped her chin up. "Well, okay then. I am glad I could help."

Holding up a plastic evidence bag containing the wicked looking knife that he had found on Valdez, Ramirez said, "I'm hoping we find traces of our victim's blood and DNA on this. That will seal our case."

"I hope so too." She twisted the water bottle cap off, and tipped back the remains. Returning the prisoner's vengeful glare, she added, "I wouldn't want to have to hurt him again."

"Bitch!" Yanking on his handcuffs, Valdez kicked at the metal seat. "You'll get yours," he shouted.

"I don't think Señor Valdez likes me very much," Maricruz said to Ramirez.

Tormenta Isla

Ramirez was still laughing and shaking his head when he climbed into the police cruiser. He stuck his arm out the driver's window and waved goodbye to Maricruz. Driving away he glanced sideways at Alexis' tight expression. Oh, yes, he was definitely going to get an earful about the pretty teniente.

Chapter 38

September 12th

Valdez slumped against the concrete wall, attempting to rest while his half-closed eyes tracked his cell mates. There were six tough men locked in an area designed for two prisoners. The hardest ones had already claimed the two narrow bunk beds, each covered with a thin pad and one filthy blanket. He and the three others snarled over the remaining space on the floor, away from the foul-smelling toilet.

The municipal police had handed him over to the State Police when it was discovered that he was wanted in connection with two other murders, one in Cancun and one in Playa del Carmen. All three murders were under the jurisdiction of the state cops and he had been transported to the larger Cancun jail yesterday morning. On the short drive from the car ferry terminal to the jails he noticed that the hurricane had just skimmed over the city, causing some damage but nothing like what had been anticipated.

At the jail his distinctive gold, lion-head ring had disappeared from his hand shortly after being transferred. He had foolishly hoped to use it to pay for his escape, or at least a better cell and edible food. Instead the processing officer had pulled the ring from his hand, telling him it would be safely stored until his trial. Whenever the hell that might be, he thought glumly.

He had been offered one call, which he used in an attempt to contact Don Rafael. Instead the phone was answered by Alfonso, the Don's bodyguard, who promised to pass his message along. It was worrisome that the drug lord had not yet responded to his plea for help. He didn't have money to buy decent food so he was forced to consume the only grub offered to prisoners; a thin gruel of water and onions, poorly cooked beans, unidentifiable meat, and quite likely a cockroach or two.

"Valdez!" a guard yelled. "Stand up, turn around and put your hands through the slot."

He ambled slowly to his feet and grudgingly complied with the shouted orders. He couldn't show fear or his roommates would use him for their personal entertainment.

The cell door clanged open. The guard grabbed Valdez's elbow and jerked him into the hallway. The second man slammed the metal grill closed with a jarring thud, then slapped his baton across Valdez's shoulders. "Move it!"

Valdez was roughly pushed inside a small airless room, with a metal table and three chairs bolted to the unpainted concrete floor. His escorts shoved him into the single chair and added a second pair of cuffs to lock his hands to the ring in the centre of the table. He tried to lean back, to pretend he was relaxed but discovered he could only rest his elbows on the scarred metal surface. He stared impassively at the two empty chairs facing him. One uniformed guard leaned against the wall the other stood outside the door.

Two more men arrived to fill the tiny space with additional body heat and the smell of sweat mixed with the odors of soap, deodorant, and a liberal dose of cologne. The older man's face was rumpled by stress and time. The younger one's was expressionless and cold.

Dressed in dark suits, white shirts and black ties, Valdez assumed they were the detectives tasked with obtaining a confession from him in any way possible. Valdez seldom had the time or money to spend on movies, but that ridiculous film Men in Black came to mind as he watched the cops.

The older man tossed a plastic bag on the table with a dirty knife sealed inside. "I'm Detective Marco Cervera. This is my partner Detective Dante Toledo." the man said flicking his index finger in the direction of the younger blank-faced man.

"Do you recognize that?" Toledo asked, pointing at the folding knife.

Valdez stared coldly at the man.

"This is the blade that the Isla Mujeres policiá found in your pocket. It has your fingerprints on it," Cervera said.

Valdez remained silent.

"According to our lab guys, those dark stains are blood. They are already running DNA tests while we have our little chat," Toledo smirked.

"Then they will compare with the results to the body of the taxi driver that was found on Isla Mujeres," Cervera said.

Valdez shrugged. It was obvious to him that these two cops had worked together many times. Lobbing their allegations back and forth, their timing was perfect, not interrupting each other just adding layer upon layer to the damning information.

"We recently found a badly mutilated corpse in the city dump," Cervera said, "after all the fancy knife work his own mother wouldn't have recognized him." The cop waited a moment, then added, "The coroner says it was a slow and painful death."

Valdez could feel his chest muscles tighten with anxiety. It had to be Sánchez.

"Lucky for us the killer left the victim's identification in his pocket, as if he wanted everyone to know the guy's name."

Cervera nodded in agreement, "Si, I think the killer was sending a message to someone," he said, flicking a cold grin at Valdez.

"It was a warning, for sure," Toledo agreed.

"I think you know him," Cervera said, "except that should be past tense ... I think you knew him."

"Fernando Sánchez," Toledo said staring watchfully at Valdez.

Valdez had guessed correctly. So that's why Don Rafael wasn't responding to his message. The man was furious, and now his own life wasn't worth spit.

"Tell us why you killed Ricardo Villarreal," Cervera said, "Maybe we can help you out a bit."

"You can't do squat for me," Valdez muttered, beads of sweat popping on his forehead.

"So, someone with a long reach hired you?"

"More power than you can possibly imagine," Valdez spat the answer at the cop, then immediately regretted giving him even the smallest crumb of information.

Toledo's eyebrows flicked up in a question as he looked at his senior partner.

Cervera tilted his chin in agreement.

"Rafael Fernandez," stated Toledo.

Surprized the cops had so quickly guessed the right name, Valdez blinked and glanced down.

"I knew it!" Toledo put his hand out, and Cervera begrudgingly pulled out his wallet, making a big show of handing over a hundred peso note.

"Do you two regularly practice your comedy routine?" Valdez asked bringing his eyes up to glare at the younger man.

Toledo reached across and slammed Valdez's face onto the metal surface. "Oh dear, I guess you tripped."

Valdez slowly raised his head, blood dripping onto the table from his nose and mouth. He ran his tongue over his lips and teeth, holding the cop's gaze as he pretended to savour the taste of his own blood.

Cervera's phone vibrated in his pocket. Cancun's electricity, cell phone and internet service had been restored a few days ago. The city was back up and running in a semi-normal manner. He pulled it out and swiped the screen. It was a text from their Captain telling them to report to him. ASAP. He handed his phone to Toledo to read the message then pointed his chin at the uniformed guard, "Take him back to his cell. We'll continue our chat later."

One guard gripped Valdez's arm while the other unlocked the set of handcuffs securing him to the table, then they marched him back to the cells. Drops of blood, dripping at regular intervals from his nose, marked his route.

The guard who had been inside the interview room leaned close to Valdez's ear and snidely whispered, "Don't close your eyes even for a second, Valdez. Don Rafael has many friends inside who consider it an honour when he asks them to tidy up a mess - free of charge."

Chapter 39

September 13th

Hands tucked in his pockets Detective Cervera stood gazing down at the naked body of Valdez. He had been found by a guard forty minutes ago in the prison's communal showers. He'd long ago become immune to death and dead bodies were never pretty, but naked dead bodies had zero dignity. He hadn't liked Valdez when he was alive. He was just a low-life killer and drug pusher but dying naked in jail was an undignified way to go.

"Well, hell. That didn't take long," Cervera said, rubbing his prickly chin. He had been asleep when the dispatcher had called, and he hadn't taken the time to shave before responding.

"He lasted less than twenty-four hours, by my estimation," agreed Toledo. He squatted to get a better look. "His neck is at an odd angle. Looks like someone twisted it."

"Looks like it. The coroner will confirm that for us." Cervera leaned one shoulder against the wall then his eyes skimmed the filth encrusted tiles, visualizing the billions of germs crawling towards his clothes. He straightened and moved away, "I really thought he'd roll over on Fernandez."

"Si, I thought we had him," Toledo agreed.

"He looked nervous at the end, sweating and avoiding eye-contact."

"We shouldn't have stopped the interrogation."

"Captain's orders," Cervera said as his eyes met Toledo's. Partners for three years they had on several occasions enjoyed a glass or two of Patrón in the privacy of their homes, while they quietly discussed who might be on the Don's payroll, and who they could trust. At times they wondered why they even cared.

"The timing sucks," Toledo grumbled.

"Claro."

"After the doc has a look, I'll update Ramirez on Isla Mujeres," Toledo said, "He's going to be angry, but he asked to be kept in the loop."

~

Ramirez's cell phone vibrated against his chest. About to start today's twenty-four hour shift his hand rested on the handle of his police vehicle. He glanced across the roof of the cruiser and caught Alexis' eye. He signalled with his thumb and forefinger, *momentito*, the wait-a-minute gesture, then pulled his phone from his pocket and read the screen.

It was from a number he didn't recognize. He was wary of unknown callers, but in his line of work it was necessary at times to give out his personal cell number. Sometimes a witness would remember more details of a crime when they had time to calm down and think about the incident.

"Bueno?" he said listening for background noises. He could hear the rush of traffic, and a car horn that honked once. Whoever was calling was near a busy street.

"Hola Ramirez. This is Detective Toledo from the State Policiá in Cancun."

"Hola, Toledo. What can I do for you?" he could feel his pulse increase a little, anticipating the state cop had already obtained a confession from Valdez.

"Bad news. Your suspect is dead."

"What?" Ramirez demanded. His free hand shot up head height, as if Toledo could see his frustrated gesture. He turned and walked a few feet away from the others. Until he knew where this conversation was headed he didn't want anyone overhearing his words. Alexis was not a problem, but the other two constables were young, inexperienced, and prone to repeating gossip to their friends and families. It was a disciplinary problem he would have to sort out another day.

"The coroner says someone broke his neck this morning while he was showering," Toledo answered.

"Definitely not an accident then?" he asked, letting his eyes roam over the police impound lot as he listened. He was alert, aware of his surroundings. Isla was a safe place to live and work, but an experienced cop learned never to completely relax.

"No, there's no soap for him to slip on," Toledo said with a grim laugh. He was referring to the standard excuse for jailhouse injuries of prisoners.

"You get anything from him?"

Toledo hesitated, then answered quietly, "We think he was hired by Rafael Fernandez."

"Think?" Ramirez asked.

"Know. But that information won't be included in our reports."

Ramirez silently thought about the message that Toledo was sending him. Someone in their office was feeding Fernandez information. That also could explain why the detective was outside making the phone call and not at his desk where he might be overheard.

"Okay. Thanks for the update," Ramirez said.

"Sure, any time." Toldeo paused, then added, "watch your back."

They said goodbye and Ramirez ended the call. He thoughtfully stared at the device. Fernandez's influence now seemed to include his little piece of paradise. *Damn drugs and the stupid people that used them.*

~

Tucking her cell phone back into her bra, Jessica turned to Yasmin, "Got a minute, chica?" she asked, pointing towards Carlos' office at the Loco Lobo.

Yasmin's glance skimmed the restaurant and she nodded. The few customers they had seemed content for the time being. "Sure. Be right there." She lifted the staff-only barrier, shutting it behind as she glided through the opening.

Jessica poked her head into Carlos' office, "Hey boss, can we come in for a minute?"

"Sure, of course," he said, rubbing his eyes. "I could use a break from this paperwork."

Yasmin smiled when she saw the familiar gesture. He needed reading glasses but was concerned they made him look old, so he refused to wear them.

Closing the door Yasmin asked, "What's up Jess?"

"Maricruz just called me. She had a phone call earlier today from Sargent Ramirez. He wanted her to know that the guy she captured was killed in the Cancun jail."

"Wow that was quick. How did the guy die?" Carlos asked.

"He wouldn't say, but she said he mentioned a cartel connection." Jessica replied.

"But why would a police officer pass along sensitive information to a Navy officer?" Yasmin asked. "Wouldn't they be reluctant to admit a prisoner had died while in custody?"

Jessica shrugged.

"Ramirez knows the Navy is working hard to prevent drugs coming onto the island." Carlos replied, "We've all seen the drug-sniffing dogs and their handlers greeting travellers as they disembark the passenger and car ferries."

"Si, claro," Yasmin said, "I've even seen them greet private yachts when the captains are checking in with the harbour master."

"They try their best, but the drugs still find their way onto the island," he said.

"Maricruz also said Ramirez warned her, and us to be extra cautious."

"Why?" Carlos asked.

Ramirez is concerned that anyone involved with the recovery of Villarreal's body, or the capture of Valdez, might be a target for the drug lord's anger," Jessica answered. "Apparently he is a nasty, volatile man."

Carlos drummed his pen on his desk, then aimed his searching gaze on Yasmin. She could see the wheels turning in his head, remembering the events of this past year. In November she had been threatened by a man who was wanted in the USA in connection with several murders, and then on New Year's Eve, Carlos had been kidnapped. It had been a very stressful year.

"We'll be fine, mi amor," she said, in a soft voice.

He stood up and wrapped his arms around her, pulling her into a tight embrace. "I adore you," he whispered.

Chapter 40

September 16th - midnight

Viva! Viva México!

Viva! Viva México!

Viva! Viva Mexico!

Jessica let the sensation wash over her. A tingle spread through her chest and ran up her arms. It just never got old, listening to thousands of proud nationals shouting: Long Live Mexico!

The square in Centro was still looking a bit ragged from being battered by Hurricane Pablo. Buildings needed paint. Some of the windows in surrounding complexes were still boarded up, but the square had been swept clean and decorated for the celebration.

They had lights, music, fireworks, cold beer, tequila, and hot food. Small flags fluttered in everyone's hands. Many islanders were dressed in an eclectic mix of anything green, white, and red - the colours of the Mexican national flag. As much as she enjoyed the company of Sparky and Max, she had left her boys safely locked inside her house. After every celebration a handful of dog owners would post photos and descriptions on Facebook of their pets that were missing. The fireworks and loud music overwhelmed the dogs' keen hearing, frightening them into running away from the painful noises.

It wouldn't be an all-nighter like New Year's Eve or the Saturday night dance during Carnaval, but it was a fiesta and people were celebrating. They had survived. No one had died because of the hurricane.

The two men, Edgar Valdez and Fernando Sánchez, who had murdered the taxi driver Ricardo Villarreal, had later been killed on orders from the Cancun drug lord who had hired them. It was a big city problem that had briefly touched their peaceful lives.

Yasmin and Carlos had their arms wrapped around each other's waists. Yasmin's parents, sister, nephews and brother-in-law were all close by, as were Carlos' mom and dad, siblings and their families. Diego and Cristina plus their four kids, and Cristina's parents formed another tight-knit and happy group of people. Even Pedro had finally found the courage to ask Maricruz for a date. She looked stunning in her bright red dress, her dark hair flowing loosely around her shoulders. It was hard to believe this was the same tough, no-nonsense Navy lieutenant who could handle a decomposing corpse and run down a criminal. She was the island's Wonder Woman.

Tormenta Isla

Jessica sighed deeply. She wished, yet again, her parents and brothers were here to share the vibe. It was her twenty-seventh birthday and Mexico was celebrating with her. For the first time ever she had bought herself an extravagant present. It was a second-hand golf cart battered by the hurricane and in need of repairs, but still functioning. It gave her the freedom to visit friends, run errands and transport her two dogs for a cooling swim in the ocean. To do what she wanted whenever she wanted. Today she was celebrating her independence as well as her birthday.

With his arm around her shoulders Luis felt her sigh and gave her a gentle squeeze. "Everything okay?" he asked.

"Si. I was just thinking about my family in Canada and how much I miss them," she said, smiling at him. "I love living on Isla, and I so want to share the experience with them."

Luis was about to say something more when Carlos caught Jessica's eye pulling her attention away.

Carlos glanced from her to Yasmin, then back at her.

She tipped her head. Yes, now.

Carlos held Yasmin's hand and he slowly sank to one knee while gazing at her shocked face.

Tormenta Isla

"Yasmin Medina will you marry me?" he held a small black velvet box in the palm of his left hand.

El Finito

About the author

Born in a British Columbia Canada gold mining community that is now essentially a ghost town, Lynda has had a very diverse working career. Her employment background has included a bank clerk, antique store owner, ambulance attendant, volunteer firefighter, supervisor of a cutting edge SkyTrain transit control centre, partner in a bed & breakfast, partner in a micro-brewery, and finally a hotel manager.

The adventure and the experience were always far more important than the paycheque.

Writing has always been in the background of her life, starting with travel articles for a local newspaper, an unpublished Great Canadian Novel written before her fortieth birthday, and articles for an American safety magazine.

When she and her husband, Lawrie Lock, retired to Isla Mujeres, Mexico in 2008, they started a weekly blog, Notes from Paradise – Isla Mujeres, to keep friends and family up to date on their newest adventure.

Needing something more to keep her active mind occupied, Lynda and island friend, Diego Medina, self-published a bi-lingual book for children, The Adventures of Thomas the Cat / Las Aventuras de Tómas el Gato. The book

Tormenta Isla

won Silver at the 2016 International Latino Book Awards for best bi-lingual picture book for children.

Well, one thing led to another and here we have Tormenta Isla, Book #3 of the Isla Mujeres Mystery Series.

Hola amigos y amigas

Pardon my Spanish, or lack of. I keep trying to learn, but every night while I am sleeping the words leak out of my brain and onto the pillow.

In a perfect world I would have written this story in Spanish or in this case Isla-Spanish which is a colourful mix of local expressions and a bit of Mayan tossed in for added flavour.

However, most of my readers are English speaking. So for the purpose of this story the local folks are fluent in both Spanish and English, especially the cuss words because aren't those the ones that we learn first in any new language?

I chose to *italicise* only a few of the less familiar Spanish expressions. I had originally *italicised* all of the Spanish but the effect was too cluttered for my eye.

For my American fans you will probably notice I spell some words differently. I use the British-Canadian words that I grew up with instead of the American version.

And as every indie writer will tell you, I rely heavily on personal recommendations and reviews to sell my books. If you enjoyed reading any of my novels, *Treasure Isla*, *Trouble Isla*, and now *Tormenta Isla* please leave a review on Amazon, Goodreads, Kobo, B&N Nook, iTunes, Bookbub, Smashwords,

Facebook or Twitter. It would mean the world to Sparky, Max and I.

Sparky is a pure-bred, island beach dog who invited himself into our lives in 2013. He walked into our house at dinner time, and never left. He has curly terrier fur covering pink and black polka-dotted skin and long silky Spaniel ears. His front paws are larger than his back ones and his sense of smell is extraordinary.

Max, our second dog, became part of our family in May of 2017. He is another island terrier-mix who is probably a twenty-seventh cousin of Sparky. Due to Lawrie's recent medical diagnosis Maxie has had to be re-homed. The lucky boy found a new and loving family near Phoenix, Arizona. We miss the little guy, but life doesn't always happen the way we plan.

If you come across an annoying blunder please email me at: lock.lynda@gmail.com and I will make it disappear with my magic keyboard.

You can also find us at various social media sites:

Facebook Lynda L Lock
Twitter Isla Mysteries
Instagram Isla Mysteries
Amazon Lynda L Lock
Bookbub Lynda L Lock
Goodreads Lynda L Lock

Acknowledgements

As many of our favourite novelists have written in their acknowledgements, writing is a solitary obsession, with hours spent creating, considering, and correcting the words on the computer screen.

However, I have had assistance from some amazing people.

Captain Tony Garcia for the beautiful photos on the covers of my all of novels plus the photo of Sparky and me at the end of the books. He is also a valuable source of information about island life.

Carmen Amato, mystery writer and creator of the *Emilia Cruz Detective Series,* re-designed the covers for both *Treasure Isla* and *Trouble Isla*, and assisted with the cover design for *Tormenta Isla*.

Our good friends Diego Medina and Jeff McGahee patiently tweaked and re-tweaked the cover for *Tormenta Isla* until I was happy with the results. One of these days I am going to learn to use Photoshop and stop pestering my friends with plaintive requests for their help.

Freddy Medina and Eva Velázquez are close friends who are always willing to share their stories of island life, this time recounting their experiences during hurricanes Gilberto and Wilma.

Tormenta Isla

Apache (Isauro Martinez Jr.) another one of my go-to-friends when I am searching for specific information about the island. For this book he told about the car ferry and Captain Hook boats that are usually moored across the entrance to the lagoon during a hurricane.

Sue McDonald Lo for sharing her notes written shortly after Wilma in 2005.

Rose-Marie Canic Zwieg a fellow Canadian who mentioned the story about a lightning strike melting a telephone.

Azatlan Association is an excellent source of information about the salinas and Maya salt trade.

Rae Clare is also a source of information about the salinas and the island women gathering salt.

The kind people who helped Max survive on the streets and after being run over in January 2017 include Tommy and Allison Merandi, Sylvie Staines, Eileen Regn, Doctor Delfino Guevera, H.A.L.O. (Helping Animals Living Overseas) and of course his new family Dianne Stocks and Willow.

The mattress incident did happen. Sparky and I saved the day.

Manuscript and proofreaders include, Lawrie Lock, Linda Grierson, Richard Grierson, Rob Goth, Julie Andrews Goth, Sue Lo, Betsy Snider, Janet Cummins, Déanne Gray, and

Tormenta Isla

Janice Carlisle Rodgers. I truly appreciate your helpful suggestions and corrections. Any and all remaining errors are my responsibility.

There are four other groups of people I would like to thank for their continuing encouragement and support:

- Faithful readers of our weekly blog, Notes from Paradise - Isla Mujeres;
- Supporters of my children's book, The Adventures of Thomas the Cat;
- Fans of my first two books of the Isla Mujeres Mystery series, Treasure Isla and Trouble Isla.
- And our island friends, ex-pats and born-here-locals who patiently answered my questions about this and that and everything.

Thank you, thank you, and thank you all!

Cheers Lynda, Sparky and Max

Tormenta Isla

Golf carts – the best way to tour the island

Indio's Isla Mujeres Golf Cart Rentals – Avenida Rueda Medina between Lopez Mateos and Matamoros in Centro *(Always our first choice for rentals!)*

Ciro's – Avenida Guerrero

Coco – Avenida Rueda Medina, next to Jax's Bar & Grill

Easy – Calle Zazil Ha, near the Lima's hotels

El Sol – Avenida Juarez, next to Hotel Kinich

Fiesta – Avenida Rueda Medina, beside the HSBC bank

Garrafon – Avenida Guerrero beside the Hotel Boca Iglesia, across from the church

GoMar – Avenida Rueda Medina across from Ultramar, in the Hotel GoMar

GoMar II – Avenida Francisco I. Madera, across from Mexico Divers

Islander – north end of Rueda Medina, near Privilege Aluxes Hotel

Tormenta Isla

Joaquin – Rueda Medina and Nicolas Bravo
Avenues (I think)

Kayla – across from basketball court in Centro

Luxury – North end of Avenida Hidalgo near
IxChel condos

North Beach Rentals – Avenida Guerrero near
Ruben's Restaurant

Pepe's – Avenida Hidalgo

Prisma – Rueda Medina

Driving a golf cart in paradise!

It sounds easy. Just point the front end, stomp on the gas and off you go on your self-guided tour of Isla Mujeres.

Caritos de golf aren't fast and are relatively easy to steer depending on the overall condition of the vehicle. Uneven pavement, unmarked pot holes, or the numerous speed bumps, called topes, can jostle a poorly maintained cart from side to side.

A typical golf cart is just darn basic. It comes equipped with four wheels, a steering wheel, seats front and back and a one-cylinder seven-horsepower gas engine. They don't have turn signals, brake lights, windshield wipers and of course, no seat belts, airbags, or baby seats. In the slightly upgraded models a horn is included and if you are lucky it might actually work.

When driving indicate your movements, lane changes, and direction changes clearly. Your arms are the turn signals. Your left arm held straight out means, hopefully, that you are turning left and not pointing out the sights to your passengers or waving to a friend. However in Mexico it can also mean that you are signalling the driver behind to pass you, so be careful what you do with that arm. Indicate your intention, check over your shoulder, look forward, and then re-check your left side again! Moto drivers like to sneak past just as you make your turn.

Your right arm or your passenger's right arm can be used to indicate a turn in that direction. The internationally recognized signal of your left arm bent at a ninety degree angle to indicate a right turn means absolutely nothing to the local folks. They think you are being friendly, and will wave back. (We've had it happen to us!)

The most important accessory on a carito de golf is the rear view mirror. Make sure your rental cart has one, and use it to frequently check for following traffic. If you want to use the mirror fix your hair or examine your teeth for leftover bits of lunch, pull over and stop.

Drive as far to the right-hand side of the lane as you safely can because other drivers will pass on corners, hills or wherever there is a little bit of space. If you are hogging the lane drivers will become impatient and pass you, expecting you to move over and make room for their vehicle to squeeze by. Motos, motorcycles and scooters will try to pass on either side of you.

During the year when families are on vacations watch out for young children steering a golf cart. It's illegal! For some strange reason folks think that the streets on Isla are quiet little lanes with a few golf carts puttering along, and that it's an incredibly cute idea to teach a youngster how to aim a vehicle.

Tormenta Isla

Look again folks. There are ambulances, fire trucks, police cruisers, garbage trucks, propane trucks, or tractor-trailer units, over two thousand golf carts, plus hundreds of taxis, personal vehicles, motorcycles and bicycles all vying for limited road space. And dogs, dozens of dogs that will cross the street when and where they want without so much as a second glance at oncoming traffic.

Another challenge of driving on Isla is the abundance of drivers posing for selfies, weaving back and forth in the lane as they try for the perfect shot of themselves and friends. Add a few cervezas and margaritas and later in the afternoon we hear the ambulances whizzing past our house, responding to yet another accident involving golf carts and motos, or golf carts and taxis, or golf carts and pedestrians.

If you get into an accident you, and everyone involved, will be driven to the police station. There you will pay for the damages to the vehicle that you hit, damages to the cart that you were driving, the other persons' medical bills, your medical bills, plus a number of traffic fines that can mount up to several hundreds of dollars.

The whole process of straightening out your accident can burn up hours and hours of your vacation time. We know from personal experience after helping other folks deal with the situation. Please, don't think about leaving the island without paying for the damages. You are a long way from home, and Mexican jails won't win any Trip Advisor Awards for Excellence.

We hope you enjoy your visit to Isla Mujeres, and don't become one of the accident statistics. It's not the way to finish up your vacation in paradise.

Hasta Luego

Lynda & Lawrie

For readers who are a little Spanish-challenged

Bruja del Mar – Literally witch of the sea, Sea Witch

Carina - sweetheart

Casita – small house

Casa – house

Chucka-chucka – humorous Mayan euphemism for sex

¿Cómo está? – How are you?

Con permiso – with permission, to move around or past a person

Don or Doña – respectful title that can be used with the person's first name

Hermano – brother, or any male who is like a brother to you

Hijo de la chingada – crude curse, son of a bitch

Hola – hi or hello

Hombre – man

IxChel – Mayan goddess of fertility and healing

La Trigueña – The young local woman who Mundaca wanted to marry

Tormenta Isla

Loco Lobo – Crazy Wolf, also El Loco Lobo but one of our Mexican friends said Loco Lobo sounded better

Maldito – darn, damn

Mama - mom

Mami - mommy

Más o menos – more or less

Mi amor – my love

Mierda – swear word, shit

Motos – motor scooters, motor bikes

Niña(s) – girl or girls

Niño(s) – boy or boys, can also mean children

Papa - dad

Papi – daddy

Pendejo – swear word, Asshole

Pícaro – horndog, randy male

Que onda? – What's up?

Rapido – rapid, fast

Testamentos – wills

Tia – auntie, or an older female who is like an aunt to you

Tio – uncle, or an older male who is like an uncle to you

Topes – speed bumps

Tormenta Isla

Sparky and his writer

Made in the USA
Lexington, KY
16 May 2018